Classic adventure

In 1931, an assassin's bullet nearly ends Brock Stone's life on the day he returns home to Washington, DC to claim his inheritance. Inside his grandfather's secret library, Stone finds a map to a lost island in the center of the Bermuda Triangle! Joined by his sometimes girlfriend, investigative reporter Trinity Page, and childhood friend, mechanical genius Alex English, and ex-boxer Moses Gibbs, Stone embarks on a rollicking adventure! Enemies lurk around every corner and an island of horrors awaits at the end of the journey, where Stone must face death in the Arena of Souls!

Fans of Indiana Jones, Dane Maddock, and Doc Savage will love Brock Stone!

PRAISE FOR DAVID WOOD!

"Indiana Jones meets The Rocketeer in this thrilling, old-school adventure!" Matt James, author of *The Forgotten Fortune*

"What an adventure! A great read that provides lots of action, and thoughtful insight as well, into strange realms that are sometimes best left unexplored." Paul Kemprecos, author of *Cool Blue Tomb* and the *NUMA Files*

"Rip roaring action from start to finish. Wit and humor throughout. Just one question - how soon until the next one? Because I can't wait." Graham Brown, author of *Shadows of the Midnight Sun*

ARENA OF

SOULS

A BROCK STONE ADVENTURE

DAVID WOOD

ADRENALINE PRESS

Published by Adrenaline Press
www.adrenaline.press

Adrenaline Press is an imprint of Gryphonwood Press
www.gryphonwoodpress.com

Cover art by Drazenka Kimpel

ISBN: 978-1940095226

BOOKS BY DAVID WOOD

The Dane Maddock Adventures
Blue Descent
Dourado
Cibola
Quest
Icefall
Buccaneer
Atlantis
Ark
Xibalba
Loch
Solomon Key
Contest
Serpent
Eden Quest (forthcoming)

Dane and Bones Origins
Freedom
Hell Ship
Splashdown
Dead Ice
Liberty
Electra
Amber
Justice
Treasure of the Dead
Bloodstorm

Dane Maddock Universe
Berserk
Maug
Elementals
Cavern
Devil's Face
Herald
Brainwash
The Tomb
Shasta
Legends
Destination: Rio
Destination: Luxor
Destination: Sofia

Bones Bonebrake Adventures
Primitive
The Book of Bones
Skin and Bones
Venom

Brock Stone Adventures
Arena of Souls
Track of the Beast

Jade Ihara Adventures (with Sean Ellis)
Oracle
Changeling
Exile

Myrmidon Files with Sean Ellis
Destiny
Mystic

Jake Crowley Adventures (with Alan Baxter)
Sanctum
Blood Codex
Anubis Key
Revenant

Sam Aston Investigations (with Alan Baxter)
Primordial
Overlord
Crocalypse (forthcoming)

Stand-Alone Novels
Into the Woods (with David S. Wood)
The Zombie-Driven Life
You Suck
Callsign: Queen (with Jeremy Robinson)
Dark Rite (with Alan Baxter)

WRITING AS FINN GRAY

The Aquaria Series
Aquaria Falling
Aquaria Burning
The Gate

WRITING AS DAVID DEBORD

The Absent Gods Trilogy
The Silver Serpent
Keeper of the Mists
The Gates of Iron

The Impostor Prince (with Ryan A. Span)
Neptune's Key

1– THE MARK

"He's just a kid," Stumpy muttered. "If he's seen thirty, I'll eat my hat." His hand drifted to his hip, and the solid comfort of the Colt .45 secreted under his jacket. Once he got close enough to his mark, he'd fill the wheat with air. There was no question the guy was a wheat: no hat, no jacket, no belt, loose-fitting shirt worn open at the neck. He was as out of place in the big city as anyone Stumpy had ever seen.

He lowered his head, tipped his hat forward, and moved with the crowd that scurried along B Street. He'd heard tell the government was going to rename it Constitution Avenue, but it would always be B Street to him. He liked things simple. The people around him seemed intent on their business, and none would have any reason to take notice of one more plainly dressed man in a group of many, and that suited him just fine. Hide in plain sight; that was the ticket.

The sky turned gray, and thunder rumbled in the distance. The scent of rain lay heavy on the cool breeze, and the people around Stumpy quickened their pace. But not his mark. He strolled along as if he hadn't a worry in the world, his blond head and broad shoulders sticking up above the throng of humanity. His size might pose a problem in a tussle though Stumpy could handle himself all right, but the convincer on his hip rendered the point moot.

"Brock Stone," Stumpy muttered. "Rich orphan, football hero, army washout. Where have you been the past two years?"

Stone suddenly left the sidewalk and headed across the Mall in the direction of the Lincoln Memorial. Stumpy had to double-time it to keep pace, so long were Stone's legs and so great was the distance eaten up with each long stride. He uttered a curse. Of the many types of people he despised, tall men were, fittingly, at the top of the list. The next time a dame in a gin mill told him, "Sorry, you're too short," he was going to burn the place down.

Stone navigated the throngs of tourists and climbed the steps up to the gleaming marble monument without breaking stride. Stumpy found a spot in the shelter of a nearby tree where he could keep an eye on Stone. On the steps, he might be noticed, and that was no good. His orders were clear: follow him, learn what you can, and then ice him when the time is right. Besides, why climb all those steps if he didn't have to?

He leaned back against the tree, drew a rolled newspaper from his inside jacket pocket, opened it to the front page, and held it just high enough that he could peer over the top. The headline screamed CAPONE PLEADS GUILTY, but the article held no interest for Stumpy. He had a feeling the judge wasn't about to accept the slap on the wrist Capone had negotiated with prosecutors. No sir. Making an example of gangsters was a big thing these days.

Stone didn't remain at the top of the memorial for very long. He descended the steps and headed back toward B Street. Stumpy tossed his paper into a nearby bin and returned to stalking his quarry.

Some men might feel conspicuous walking armed down a crowded street, following a man who would be dead by sunset, but not Stumpy. He was completely at home in this warren of crowded streets and tall buildings. The lion had its savanna, the tiger its jungle, and Stumpy had the city. At moments like this, he could almost imagine himself to be the angel of death.

Except Stumpy got paid a lot better.

A forked tongue of lightning split the sky and thunder boomed like cannon fire. Everyone flinched at the sound. Everyone except Stumpy... and Stone.

"Do you have nerves of steel, or are you just a twit?" Stumpy found himself growing more and more curious as he stalked his prey. Understanding the man you were going to kill was important— it helped you predict his actions, but for Stumpy, it was more than that. There was something about taking a life that bonded you with that person in an intimate way. It was the closest to spirituality he ever came; Christmas and Easter mass included.

"I'll know more about you once I put this baby into action." He patted the flat, rectangular package tucked into his belt just to make sure it was still there. He'd never used it before, but his employer had explained how it worked, and it seemed simple enough.

The first drops of rain spattered the street and a forest of umbrellas sprouted in response. Suddenly, Stone was not so easy to see. Stumpy quickened his pace and caught sight of the big man as he disappeared into an office building. The sign on the front read *Edgar Porter and Associates, Attorneys At Law.* Stumpy had learned that Stone's parents had passed away a few years back while Stone was in the army, right about the time

Stone seemingly disappeared from the face of the earth. Probably he was here about his inheritance.

Stumpy hurried to the front door and paused. It would be a close thing. If Stone spotted him, Stumpy would have to end things right there, and that meant a major cut in pay. The deal was simple: half for the information, half to put an end to the big man. He caught the door with his heel, and leaned against the wall, pretending to take respite from the rain beneath the tiny awning, and strained his ears to listen.

"May I help you?" a silky, feminine voice asked.

"Brock Stone. I have an appointment." Stone's words were curt, but his tone was polite, if not friendly.

"Yes, sir. Mister Porter will be meeting with you personally. Second floor. You'll see his door when you reach the top of the stairs. He's expecting you, so feel free to go right in."

Stumpy dared a glance inside. Stone was climbing the stairs and the secretary, a doll with chestnut hair and curves in all the right places, stared after him with a look akin to hunger in her brown eyes. No way he'd be able to slip past her. A quick glance up the steps told him that Porter's office was on the back side of the building. He'd try there first and see how it shook out.

His feet clopped on the wet pavement as he ducked through an alley and circled around to the back of the building. Winded, he took a moment to catch his breath as he scanned the back face of the law office. Unlike its marble facade, the back wall was red brick, with an iron fire escape running to the roof. Perfect!

Stumpy took out the rectangular package, a small case the size of a book. He unsnapped the end flap, and withdrew a tiny box with an antenna and cuplike attachment, and flicked the switch on the bottom. A green light flickered to life, telling him the transmitter was live. Next, he withdrew an earpiece on a coiled wire, inserted it in his ear, and plugged it into the device inside the leather box. Finally, he flipped a switch. Static crackled in his earpiece, and the recorder inside began to whir. Satisfied, he crept up the fire escape.

Porter's office was typical for a rich guy: oversized and ostentatious. Through one of the half-dozen windows, he saw the attorney, a bear of a man with glasses and thinning hair, seated behind a mahogany desk, facing Stone, who sat ramrod-straight in a leather chair. Cautiously, Stumpy pressed the cup to the window pane, turned it until it stuck, and drew away from the window. Through the earpiece, he could hear the men's conversation, the sound tinny and hollow, but the words clear as a nice glass of gin.

"If you don't mind my saying, you're a difficult man to reach, Mister Stone."

"I've been traveling out of the country for some time. I only returned a few days ago. That's when I received your letters."

"I understand. I fear I have bad news. Your grandfather passed away three weeks ago."

So this *was* about an estate, but not that of Stone's parents. Stumpy listened with keen interest.

"How did it happen?" Stone's voice betrayed no emotion, but when Stumpy stole a glance through the window, sadness painted the young man's strong face and flooded his downcast brown eyes.

"I only know it was sudden. The doctors do not believe he suffered." A brief pause, the whisper of shuffling papers,

and Porter went on. "My instructions are to give these to you. It's your inheritance, though I'm given to understand there's very little money in the estate."

"Money I have. My parents left me everything."

"You've had more than one loss in the past few years."

"More than you know." The sound of tearing paper, and Stone uttered a confused grunt. "He's left me his mansion on the Potomac and a copy of The Lost World."

"That's a fine bequest," Porter said. "I've been to the mansion. It's but a stone's throw from Mount Vernon and offers a beautiful view of the river."

"It's a dust and cobweb-filled rat trap," Stone said. "My grandfather seldom ventured above the first floor. More than once, I asked him why he held on to the place, but he would just laugh and say he needed a house large enough to hold all his secrets."

"I assume the book holds some significance?"

"It was my favorite book as a child. I lost count of how many times I made him read it to me." Stone cleared his throat. "Mister Porter, I neither want nor need the mansion. Can you see to its disposal?"

"What do you mean?"

"Sell it, give it away, burn it to the ground for all I care. My parents' house in Alexandria is more than enough for me."

"I think that would be a mistake." Porter spoke slowly. "Your grandfather made a point to impress upon me the importance of you assuming ownership of the mansion. I've never seen him so insistent."

"Did he say why?"

"He said I should insist that you sit in the window

seat and read the book one last time, whatever that means."

"I know what he means, but I'll be hanged if I understand his reasons. I suppose I should get this over with. Thank you for your time, Mister Porter. I'll be in touch."

Stumpy switched the recorder to the *Off* position, removed the earpiece, and set it on the fire escape. He would learn no more from this meeting. Drawing his Colt, he moved back to the window. It was time to close the deal.

2- THE BUG

Brock Stone stood and reached out to shake Porter's hand. The attorney rose to his full height, almost at eye level with Stone's six feet, two inches, and clasped Stone's hand. Although he worked behind a desk, the attorney's grip was strong. Stone opened his mouth to bid Porter goodbye, but paused when a flicker of movement at the window caught his eye.

"Down!" Stone leapt forward, vaulting the desk and crashing into Porter as the window exploded and the sound of two gunshots in quick succession filled the air. The two men fell in a heap on the floor. Moving fast for a man of his size, Porter scrambled for the shelter of the desk, a bullet pinging off the hardwood floor only inches from his heel.

Stone rolled to the side, grabbed a heavy wooden wastebasket, and hurled it at the shattered window. It struck the surprised attacker on the wrist, sending his next shot upward. Plaster rained down as the bullet cracked the ceiling. A side table followed the wastebasket. Stone was a powerful man, his muscles honed by years of football, military service, and the training he'd done on his own in the time since. The table cracked the attacker across the forehead as another bullet went astray.

Stone's assailant, a barrel of a man, carried a Colt 1911. Assuming he'd begun with a full magazine and one round in the chamber, he still had three shots left. His face a crimson mask from the gash on his forehead; the man looked around for Stone, who sprang to the side and pressed against the wall, inches from the window frame, waiting.

Stone strained to hear movement over the patter of rain. A foot scraped on metal, perilously close, and then the barrel of the Colt appeared in the window.

Stone grabbed the weapon in his left hand, yanked it forward, and struck out with the back of his right fist. The man cried out in pain as Stone's hard strike crushed the bridge of his nose. He reeled backward, instinctively pulling the trigger as he stumbled.

Stone released the weapon as it discharged, and the man seized that moment to flee. Footsteps pounded on the fire escape, and Stone sprang to the window to give pursuit. He was halfway out when a bullet pinged off the window facing inches from his head.

"Wait!" Strong hands hauled Stone back inside. Porter had pulled him back. "You can't chase him down the fire escape," Porter said. "You'll be far too exposed. If he has a spare magazine, you'll be like a target in a shooting gallery."

Stone doubted the assailant would have fled, had he been carrying spare ammunition. In any case, it wasn't in his nature to run from a fight. He shook free of Porter's grip and returned to the window in time to see his attacker dashing down the alleyway. The attorney had slowed Stone enough to let the man get a good head start.

"I'll take my chances." Stone sprang through the window, descended the fire escape three steps at a time, and took off down the alleyway, splashing through puddles as he ran. The rain had stopped, but a haze hung in the warm evening air.

During his playing days at Virginia Military Institute, he'd seen duty as both a running back and defensive back, and had been the fastest man on the team. In seconds, he had his quarry in sight. The man was fast, considering his short legs, but Stone was faster. His powerful strides devoured the intervening space at a rapid clip.

The alley opened up onto a busy street, and the man sprinted into traffic without regard for his own safety. A bus slammed on the brakes, just missing him. The driver yanked the wheel hard to the right, and the big vehicle rode up onto the curb and came to a screeching halt, blocking the alleyway.

Undeterred, Stone hit the ground and belly crawled underneath the bus, the smell of oil and ozone heavy in the air. He was halfway across when it began backing up.

As the big tires closed in, Stone spun a quarter of a turn and rolled forward. He tumbled off the curb and into the street, the front wheel grazing his foot as it passed. Spotting him, the driver cried out in anger, but Stone was on his feet, looking around for his quarry. He saw him, silhouetted in the back of a cab as it disappeared down Virginia Avenue.

Stone had lost him.

Seething with anger, he jogged back to Porter's office, passing on the front door and instead taking the fire escape back up.

"The police are on their way," Porter said as Stone appeared in the window. He looked down at the shattered glass strewn across the floor and raised his hands. "What do you think he wanted?"

"To kill me," Stone said. "I should think that would be obvious."

"Why here? Why now?"

"For that matter, how did anyone know I was back in the country?" Stone retrieved the copy of *The Lost World* he had dropped on the floor during the attack, and turned to look out the window. The jagged shards of glass gave it the appearance of a predator's gaping maw. In the corner, an object clinging to one of the remaining slivers caught his eye.

He removed it and held it up for Porter to see.

"It's a listening device." He turned it over in his hand, scrutinizing the small box. "Fairly advanced, too. I've seldom seen its like. This tells me a few things."

Porter scratched his chin. "Such as?"

"The man I chased was likely a hired thug, working for someone with a lot of resources. Someone who didn't just want me dead, but wanted information."

"Do you think they're interested in your inheritance?"

"Perhaps." Stone pocketed the device and turned back toward the window. "The only thing I'm certain of is, I need to get to my grandfather's house as quickly as possible."

3- THE HOUSE

A shadowy figure lurked in the doorway of Stone's Alexandria townhouse. He slowed his approach, readying himself for a fight, but relaxed when the figure moved out into the moonlight.

"Alex!" Stone exclaimed.

Alex English stood six feet, four inches tall, his frizzy ginger hair making him appear even taller. He was one of the few people Stone had to look up to, though not by much. He closed the book he was reading, *The Time Machine* by H.G. Wells, and stepped out to greet Stone, his rail-thin body barely casting a shadow on the sidewalk.

"You're going to go blind reading by moonlight," Stone said, glancing at the book.

"You sound like my mother." Alex grinned, the scar on his left cheek glowing dully in the pale light. "It's been a long time."

"It has."

"Well, what are you waiting for? Slip me five." Alex offered his hand, and Stone gave it a firm shake.

"When were you planning on letting me know you were back in town?" Alex asked.

"Tomorrow. I've been busy seeing to my grandfather's estate."

"I was sorry to hear about that." Alex shivered and rubbed his arms. "Some host you are. Were you planning on inviting me in for coffee?"

"Afraid I'm not staying. I'm headed out to Riverbend." Stone paused. "My grandfather left it to me. I'm just here to arm myself."

Alex frowned. "Sounds serious. Want some company?"

"I'd welcome it, but it could be dangerous." Stone opened the door and let his friend inside. The townhouse, a short distance from the waterfront, had been in his family since its construction in 1796. His parents had furnished it with Colonial-era antiques, and it felt to Stone more like a museum than a home. He proceeded to the roll-top desk in the drawing room, where he kept his father's pistol. The Webley Top-Break revolver was of British make and the standard issue service sidearm for the British army. Stone made sure it was fully loaded with .455 cartridges, pocketed a handful of spares, and led Alex back outside. "Are you sure you want to go along?"

"I need some excitement in my life," the tall, slender man replied. "Designing advanced aircraft is interesting, but a bit too safe."

"When did you start loving danger?" Stone asked.

"Right about the time I learned you were back. I suddenly had the urge to scale a cliff, go diving, maybe even get into a fistfight."

"If we run into trouble, it will probably be worse than a fistfight. I'll tell you about it on the way."

Alex paused and looked up and down the street. "How do you plan on getting there? I didn't see you drive up."

"My cab's waiting down the street. I had the driver stop and let me out as soon as I saw someone lurking around my house."

"I see your eyesight hasn't worsened with age." Alex winked. Both men were a few years short of thirty, but Stone was two weeks older, and his friend never let him forget it. "But you can send the cabbie on his way. I'm driving." He inclined his head toward a shiny, black DeSoto CF convertible parked on the other side of the street.

"That's your car? Nice." Stone admired the sleek lines and shiny chrome.

"It's brand new, so no fingerprints on the paint job."

"You're the boss," Stone said.

As they made the short drive to Riverbend, he filled Alex in on the events of the day.

"Who might want you dead?" Alex turned off the main road and up the unmarked driveway. "Have you wronged anyone lately?"

"Not lately." Stone left it at that.

Riverbend, his grandfather's Georgian Colonial mansion, stood on a rise overlooking the Potomac. Located at the end of a winding dirt driveway, and surrounded by dense forest, the house was unknown to most. Stone gazed at the three-story brick mansion, taking comfort in its familiarity—the front door flanked by twin white columns and topped with a decorative crown, the four evenly-spaced gables set in the pitched roof, and the twin chimneys standing like sentinels at either end. All of it brought back memories of his early years.

"It doesn't look much different," Alex said, stopping in front of the closed carriage house set off to the side. "It could stand some fresh paint, but otherwise, it's the same as I remember."

Stone climbed out of the DeSoto and drank deeply of the night air. The cool breeze carried the crisp smell of freshly-mowed grass and a whiff of the Potomac to his nostrils. For the first time since he'd returned to America, he felt like he was home.

His moment of reverie evaporated as a shadow moved behind a magnolia tree on the opposite side of the circular drive.

"Get behind the car," he whispered. Drawing the Webley, he drew a bead on the shape behind the tree. Amidst the blacks and grays of the shadowy night, he could just make out the outline of a man…

… and the barrel of a rifle.

"Drop your weapon and come out with your hands on your head." He poured all the authority he could muster into the words. "Do it now, or the next and last sound you hear will be the report of my pistol."

"Technically, bullets travel faster than the speed of sound," Alex whispered from behind the shelter of the DeSoto. "At that distance…"

"Not now," Stone said out of the side of his mouth. He stifled a grin. At least one thing about Alex hadn't changed.

The man behind the magnolia slowly lowered his rifle, laid it on the ground, and raised his hands. He rounded the tree and stopped dead in his tracks when he saw Stone.

"Mister Brock?"

"Moses!" Stone lowered the revolver. "What are you doing here? And since when do you call me 'Mister?'"

Moses Gibbs was the grandson of Isaac Gibbs, Riverbend's caretaker. He and Stone had sometimes played together as children and remained friendly in their teen years, though they couldn't truly be friends, for reasons beyond their control: namely, the color of their skin.

"Since I started working for you." Moses folded his muscular arms across his chest and shifted from foot-to-foot, looking around. He nodded at Alex, who had emerged from his hiding place to stand beside Stone.

"You're still helping your grandfather? I thought you'd moved away."

"I did. Moved to New York and tried my hand at boxing for a while, but a black man can't get a better deal there than he can in Virginia. Promoter told me I had to throw a match before I could get a shot at the title. When I did, they passed me over and gave the fight to a white fighter I'd done beat. So I come back here and worked with Pappy until he died, and then I took over for him."

"I hadn't heard," Stone said. Suddenly remembering his manners, he introduced Alex.

Alex offered his hand, and Moses hesitated for only an instant before taking it. They made an odd pair—Alex pale and lean, Moses dark and solid.

"I remember you from way back," Moses said. "Don't see many men as tall as you, and not many more with hair like that."

"My friends say I look like a torch." Alex stood up straight and ran a hand through his red hair, eliciting a chuckle from Moses.

"What were you doing out here with your rifle?" Stone asked.

"Somebody done broke in, and I was checking around to make sure they was gone."

Stone's hand went back to his Webley. "I thought I had more time. This place isn't well known, nor is it easy to find if you don't know where you're going." He ignored Moses' puzzled expression. "You didn't see anyone?"

Moses shook his head. "Looked like they searched the whole downstairs. Drawers turned out; books pulled off the shelves. Made a right mess of things. I'll show you." He retrieved his rifle, led them inside, and turned on the light.

The house was not what Stone had expected. Gone were the layers of dust and the faint smell of mold. The polished wood floor shone brightly and the walls and ceilings were free of cobwebs.

"I done my best to keep things in good order," Moses said. "Pappy got to where he couldn't do much, but I've mostly got it set right. I haven't got to the upstairs yet. I even got your Scout running nice and smooth. I hope you don't mind, but I take it out from time to time. It ain't good for the engine and tires if it just sits."

"You're right about that. I appreciate you taking care of it in my absence." Stone's Indian Scout motorcycle had been his pride and joy during his college years. Suddenly, he couldn't wait to take it for a spin.

"You like to tinker?" Alex asked Moses.

"Sure do."

Alex clapped Moses on the shoulder. "You and I are going to get along just fine."

Stone raised his hand to silence them. A thought had just occurred to him.

"Moses, how do you know the intruder's not still here?"

"I done checked."

"How about the upstairs? Did you look there?"

Moses' eyes went wide. "I didn't think of it, what with all the rooms being closed off and all. There ain't nothing up there."

"He doesn't know that. I think I should check it out." Stone thought for a moment. "If he's upstairs, he'll have heard us arrive. You two wander around down here for a minute, and then go back outside. Keep talking the whole time, loud enough for him to hear, but try to make it sound natural."

"Child's play. I'm no stranger to the theater," Alex said. He and Moses began discussing the break-in in raised voices and headed back toward the kitchen.

Webley at the ready, Stone crept up the stairs, hoping his weight would not cause the old boards to creak and give him away. He paused when he reached the first landing. The light through the window shone on a single set of footprints in the dust on the steps leading upstairs. No prints led down. Of course, that didn't mean the intruder hadn't exited by way of the back staircase, but someone had definitely been here.

The footprints vanished in the darkness as Stone reached the second floor. Craning his head to the side, he strained to listen for any sound that would indicate the intruder's presence. He waited, the thrum of his heartbeat the only sound. Perhaps the man, whoever he was, had gone.

His eyes gradually adjusting to the dark, Stone stepped out into the second-floor hallway and turned to his right. He'd check the rooms just to be safe. As his hand closed around the closest doorknob, something moved behind him. He whirled about and dropped to one knee as the world erupted in a muzzle flash and the thunder of a gunshot.

4- TRINITY

Stone didn't flinch as the bullet whizzed past him. He returned fire, aiming for the spot where he'd seen the muzzle flash. He followed with two shots, one to either side, in quick succession. He guessed right with the third shot. A man's voice cried out in pain, and footsteps thudded down the hallway away from him.

Silhouetted against the floor-to-ceiling window at the end of the hall, the man's short, thick outline identified him as the same goon who had attacked Stone at the attorney's office. Hand pressed to his side, the man staggered as he ran.

Stone dashed after him, but his swift feet were not sufficient to close the gap before, with a loud crash, the goon smashed through the window and plunged into the darkness. He scarcely had time to cry out before he hit the ground with a thud. Reaching the window, Stone looked down at his quarry, hoping the fellow was still alive, so Stone could question him, but Stone could immediately tell that the fall had done him in. The man lay on the grass, his head twisted at a severe angle, limbs splayed out. He'd tell no secrets.

By the time Stone descended the stairs and reached the spot where the intruder had fallen, Alex and Moses knelt over the man, Alex's face twisted in disgust, Moses' expression unreadable.

"Who is he?" Alex whispered.

"That's what I hope to find out." Stone searched the corpse, patting it down and rifling through the man's pockets. He found only a few spare bullets and a single coin.

"This is odd." He held the coin up, letting the moonlight glint off its worn surface.

"Is that a doubloon?" Alex asked.

"Perhaps. It's unlike any I've seen before." Despite its wear, he could clearly make out the markings on the coin's surface. One side featured a warrior in an ornate headdress; the reverse, a sunburst behind a pyramid. "It's quite old, but it doesn't appear to be Spanish. In fact, it's primitive-looking. See how the edges aren't crisp?" He turned the coin around so Alex and Moses could see.

"There's no date," Alex observed.

"No value on it, either," Moses added.

Stone nodded and pocketed the coin. "That's just one mystery."

"True. We still don't know who the man is or what he wanted." Alex looked up, as if the answer lay in the sky.

"Killing Mister Brock is what he wanted. Ain't that obvious?" Moses asked.

"Moses, if you can't bring yourself to call me Brock, at least call me Stone. Whatever else you do, lose the Mister. We're friends."

Moses shifted uncomfortably but didn't argue.

"There's another mystery to unravel." Stone rose to his feet. "This man planted a listening device on the window of the attorney's office. If he was either listening or recording it, where is the other piece of the device?"

"Perhaps he only planted the bug, and someone in another building was listening in?" Alex suggested.

Stone shook his head. "I've seen this type of unit before. The range is too limited for that."

"He had to get himself here somehow," Moses said. "Might be he left it inside his car."

"When I last saw him, he was leaving in a cab. Of course, that doesn't mean he didn't retrieve his own vehicle and drive here. Would you mind scouting around?"

Moses agreed. He propped his rifle on his shoulder and disappeared into the darkness.

Alex gave Stone a long, level look.

"There's something else on your mind. What is it?"

Just then, twin beams sliced through the damp night. Stone sprang to his feet and drew his Webley. Who would come here this late in the evening, or at all for that matter? His grandfather hadn't entertained guests in ages.

"Put your gun away," Alex said. "I recognize the car."

"Who is it?"

Alex thrust his hands into his pockets and shifted his weight from foot to foot. "Don't be sore, but I told her you were back," he said in a rush. "The way you left things with her, I thought you two should talk."

"I don't have anything to say to her right now. But you and I are going to have a serious talk later."

The driver parked the car behind Alex's DeSoto and cut the engine. A woman stepped out and closed the door behind her.

The years had been good to Trinity Paige. She had realized the promise of beauty that had been evident in her youth. Stone had seen her at his parents' funeral, of course, but she had changed since then in some indefinable way. Gone was the girlish quality she'd retained well into her twenties, replaced by an air of self-assurance that Stone found striking. Suddenly, he was no longer angry with Alex for inviting her here.

He grinned as he took in her ivory skin, wavy brown hair, full lips, and fuller figure as she glided toward him…

… and slapped him across the face.

"I'll be inside." Alex hurried away, leaving Stone and Trinity staring at one another.

They stood only inches apart, but to Stone, it seemed like miles.

"You left without a word, and I don't hear from you for years." Trinity's voice, husky with emotion, still held that breathless quality that Stone found so appealing. "And then you finally come back and I have to hear it from Alex?" She gritted her teeth and drew her hand back to slap him again, but Stone grabbed her wrist.

"None of that." He felt her arm relax, and he released her wrist.

He hadn't thought to grab her other arm. Her left-handed slap sent a burst of white light flashing across his eyes and made his ear ring.

"Are you finished now?" he growled.

"I don't know. Does it hurt?"

"Of course it hurts."

"Then I'm finished. For now." She folded her arms and tapped one foot impatiently. "Explain yourself."

Stone didn't know if he could explain.

"You have to understand. It wasn't just you I left behind. I had to get away from the world, from myself, for a while." Stone's cheeks stung, but he refused to give Trinity the satisfaction of seeing him acknowledge the pain. "I was going to call you as soon as I figured out what to say."

"The truth would have been a good start. I don't know what was worse: thinking you were dead, or thinking you'd forgotten me." A single tear traced its way down her cheek. Stone reached out to brush it away, but she batted his hand aside. "No, that's not true. Of course believing you dead was worse, but you hurt me. Deeply."

"I'm sorry." He didn't know what else to say.

"That's not even close to enough, Stone. You owe me an explanation."

"I'm not sure I can explain, but I'll do my best. Right now, though, I need to deal with this." He pointed to the body lying on the ground.

Trinity seemed to notice the corpse for the first time, and flinched. "Who is he?"

"The bruno who tried to kill me. That's all I know."

"Kill you?" For a moment, Trinity's features softened, but her resolve firmed almost instantly. "I didn't hire him, if that's what you're thinking. I will admit to *considering* killing you myself, though."

"I'm glad you changed your mind."

"Don't let your guard down just yet. I haven't completely dismissed the idea." She rummaged in her purse and pulled out a pencil and pad. Her posture changed. Suddenly, she stood ramrod straight, the tip of her pencil hovering just above the paper. "So, tell me what happened here."

"What are you doing?" Stone asked.

"I'm a reporter for the *Washington Scribe,* and this is news. Do you want to tell me your side, or should I fill in the blanks myself?"

"Trinity, this is the last thing I need."

"I don't care. It'll be in the papers anyway, unless you plan on covering this up."

"Of course not. I didn't do anything wrong." Stone ran a hand through his hair. He had enough hassles without Trinity making things worse. Then again, she might be a useful ally. "I'll make a deal with you. I'll tell you about *two* attempted murders this evening. If," he paused, "you do some investigating for me."

Trinity considered this for a moment, her brown eyes boring into his. Finally, she nodded.

"Done. What am I investigating?"

5- THE BOOK

The whisper of the wind in the pines bathed the house in a soft blanket of peace, but sleep eluded Stone. Uncomfortable taking up residence in his grandfather's bedroom, he'd given it over to Alex and instead stretched out on a plush rug in the sitting room in front of the cold fireplace. Now he lay staring up at the ceiling, turning the doubloon over in his hand and rubbing his thumb across its smooth surface.

After the police had taken his and the others' statements and the morgue hauled away the intruder's body, he and Trinity had talked for more than an hour. Rather, she talked and he listened. She'd applied all her skills as a reporter to try and find out where he'd gone and what he'd done since he left the service, but he'd managed to gently rebuff her attempts without further raising her ire. She'd finally headed home, promising to pay a visit to the taxicab company the following morning and see if she could root out any information about the deceased man, and perhaps even locate the missing recording device. Relief had dueled with loneliness as he watched her drive away, but it was not thoughts of the beautiful young woman that kept him awake now.

Minutes turned to hours until finally, at three o'clock, Stone rose. He didn't need a watch. He'd always had what others considered an uncanny sense of time, but to him, it was natural. He started pacing, unable to put a finger on what bothered him. It lingered in the back of his mind like an itch he could not scratch. Giving up any hope of sleep, he headed to his grandfather's study and searched the shelves in vain for a book that might give him a clue about the doubloon: books on Spanish history, books about South and Central America and the Caribbean. Nothing.

When the first hint of dawn painted a stripe of dull gray across the eastern horizon, he headed outside, removed his shoes and socks, and walked out into the cool, damp grass. He closed his eyes, breathed deeply of the moist, clean air, and flowed into the forms that had become a part of him since he became the first Westerner to penetrate the secrets of the Shang Lau. His conscious mind focused on the movements of his arms and legs: smooth, powerful, and always perfectly balanced. Now, his subconscious mind was free to drift. It was a technique that had served him well many times, and it did not fail this time. Suddenly, he had it!

Satisfaction coursing through him, he completed the form before putting his socks and shoes back on and returning to the house. The aroma of coffee greeted him when he opened the door, and he found Alex in the kitchen, spooning sugar into a cup of light brown liquid.

"I don't know how you can stand to drink it like that," Stone said, pouring a cup for himself. "All that sugar and milk is bad for your gut."

Alex, lean as a greyhound, looked down at his flat stomach and made a face. "I think I'm all right."

"For now." Stone took a swallow of the hot, dark liquid. Alex had made it just right— heavy on the coffee grounds, light on the water.

"You were up early," Alex said.

"Correction. I'm up late."

"And you're concerned about the way I take care of myself?" Alex shook his head. "Everyone needs sleep. Even the great Brock Stone." He gestured toward Stone with his coffee cup.

"I don't need much sleep. Never have."

"Something bothering you?" Alex's face reddened. "All right, that was a foolish question. I mean, aside from the obvious."

"Yes, but it took me a while to figure it out." Stone took another swallow of coffee. "My grandfather left me all his belongings, including his books, but he made a point to have his attorney give me a copy of *The Lost World*. There has to be a reason."

Alex nodded thoughtfully. "That book was published nearly twenty years ago, and I don't remember much of the plot, but I think there's an obvious connection you're overlooking."

"What's that?"

"On the day you are given a book, from your grandfather, about the search for a lost world, a man tries to kill you. And what do we find in his pocket?"

"You think the doubloon comes from a lost civilization?" Stone removed the coin from his pocket and laid it on the kitchen table. He should have thought of it himself, but Trinity was the one person who had always been able to tie his mind into knots, and her sudden, unexpected appearance had him all out of kilter.

"Comes from… Depicts a legend of… Who knows? But it's quite a coincidence, isn't it?"

"Perhaps." Stone drained his coffee cup and waved away Alex's offer of a refill. Had his grandfather been trying to send him a message with the gift of the book? It was certainly possible. "We should search his papers. Perhaps there's something there."

They headed to the study, where Stone searched through the contents of his grandfather's desk while Alex examined the books on the shelves. Next, they checked the writing desk in the sitting room, and even the drawers in the kitchen, but found nothing. Finally, they searched the master bedroom, also without success.

"This is wrong." Stone voiced the thought that had plagued him since he'd left the study.

"What do you mean?" Alex dropped heavily onto the side of the bed.

"Think back. What do you remember about my grandfather?"

"Not much. It seemed like he always had his nose in a book, or was writing in his journal."

"Exactly. He wrote in that journal every day, sometimes several times a day. He must have filled, I don't know, two or three journal books a year."

"So?"

"Where are they?" Stone raised his arms. "For that matter, where are the rest of his books? The shelves in the study can't possibly hold even a tenth of his library."

"You think the study is a facade?" Alex scratched his chin.

"Exactly. I think his true study is hidden somewhere."

Just then, someone knocked, and then a voice called out. "Mister Brock… I mean, Stone, are you here?"

"We're in the master bedroom, Moses. Come on back."

Moments later, Moses' muscular form appeared in the doorway. "I seen the light was on and thought I'd check with you to ask if they's anything in particular you want me to attend to today."

"Actually, we could use your help. What were my grandfather's daily activities like?"

Moses considered the question. "Mostly reading and writing. He'd take a little sunshine of the morning, maybe stroll down the lane." He paused. "Can't really say what he did all day long. He disappeared for hours at a time most every day. Wouldn't see him until evening."

"Where did he go?" Stone asked.

Moses shrugged. "I always reckoned he was napping, but sometimes I'd be working outside and I'd notice his bedroom was empty."

Stone and Alex exchanged glances. It fit.

"Did he ever go into any of the outbuildings?" Alex asked. "The carriage house, perhaps?"

Moses shook his head.

"Moses, have you ever seen anything that looked like a secret doorway anywhere in the house or on the property?" Stone's heart raced. He knew he was on the right track. He just needed a clue.

Moses slowly shook his head. "Can't say that I have."

Stone sighed. His copy of *The Lost World* lay on the bedside table. He picked it up and thumbed through it. "What's your secret, Grandfather?" he muttered. Discouraged, he tossed the book back onto the table.

And froze.

"What is it?" A look of concern marred Alex's face.

"I just remembered something the attorney told me. Grandfather specifically instructed me to sit in the window seat and read this book one last time."

"So?"

Stone moved to the window seat and settled in at an

angle with his legs hanging over the edge, just like he'd always sat as a child when his grandfather read to him. He no longer fit well, but its purpose was served when he saw what lay directly in his line of sight.

"Look at that painting." He pointed across the room.

Alex turned around and his jaw dropped.

"It's the same as what's on the cover of that book," Moses marveled.

"You don't think…" Alex began.

"Yes I do." The painting, a good six feet tall and three feet wide, depicted a plateau rising above a dense jungle, and nearly reached the ceiling. "It's like the plateau described in *The Lost World*. And this painting is more than large enough to hide a doorway."

The three of them moved in lockstep. When they reached the painting, Stone took hold of the frame and pulled. It resisted, then with an audible click, swung forward, revealing a stout wooden door.

Stone smiled. "This is it."

6— THE ROOM

A cool, damp breeze wafted out of the dark doorway, carrying with it a hint of mildew. Stone ran his hand along the rough stone wall, feeling all of its imperfections. He wondered what, exactly, they had stumbled onto.

"Now this is an interesting development." Alex took a box of matches out of his pocket, struck one on the crumbling mortar between two stone blocks, and held it up. Flecks of mica in the granite wall sparkled in the flickering light, illuminating a staircase that spiraled down into the darkness. A few cobwebs clung to the ceiling. A narrow path ran through the dust on the stairs.

"I guess we know where Grandfather was going. Shall we?" Stone looked at Alex and Moses.

"How about I stay up here and keep an eye on things?" Moses asked. "Just in case whoever sent that man last night sends somebody else."

"Thank you." Stone retrieved an antique oil lamp from a shelf in his grandfather's study, lit it, and descended the steps. Winding down into the darkness, he wondered at the secret his grandfather kept hidden. Had Stone not disappeared when he had, would his grandfather have shared this place with Stone while he still lived?

"I wonder how far down it goes," Alex whispered. "We must have gone a good twenty feet already."

"Considering the age of the house, it's an impressive feat to build something so far below ground. Makes you wonder what the purpose was." Stone brushed cobwebs out of his face and kept going.

"It's far too old to have been a part of the underground railroad." Alex fell silent and paused. He stood there, stroking his chin. His gaze seemed to drift beyond their surroundings and his eyes grew misty. Finally, he shook his head. "I'm afraid I am fresh out of ideas."

"And we're fresh out of stairs. Look here." Stone halted in front of a metal door. He tried the handle and was pleased to find it unlocked. As he pushed it open, he sensed a large space on the other side. Holding his lamp out in front of him, he stepped through.

He was in an oval room that appeared to be hewn from the natural rock. The floor was perfectly smooth, and shelves and cubbyholes filled with books and other objects lined the walls, running back into the darkness beyond the circle of lamplight. Up above, soot, likely from fires centuries ago, stained the ceiling.

"It's a cave," Alex marveled.

"But it's much more than that now." Stone noticed a handle on the wall and raised it. With a heavy click, it slid into place, and a faint humming from an invisible generator filled the room as a series of electric lights slowly came to life. Bit by bit, the cavern revealed itself.

The place was much more expansive than Stone could have imagined. It was at least a hundred feet long and filled with his grandfather's treasures: books, weapons, artwork, and artifacts accumulated over a lifetime. At the far end, he could just make out several tables covered with pipes, tubes, and glass. A laboratory!

"I've never seen anything like this." As if in a trance, Alex made for the lab.

Stone headed for a large wooden desk set dead-center in the middle of the room beneath an ornate chandelier. On the way, he took note of some of the relics his grandfather had collected. There were items from all over the world and from every major culture. How had he acquired them all without anyone knowing?

On shelves nearest the desk he found his grandfather's journals, each numbered on the spine and dated on the front cover in Samuel's spidery hand. The ending date of the last volume was nearly a year ago. He supposed the answers to his question could be found in any of these, but he wanted to begin with the most recent volume, but where was it? The desktop was clear and the drawers held pens, pencils and paper, but no journal.

He looked around, trying to think like his grandfather. Where would Samuel Stone have hidden the journal? He had left *The Lost World* as a clue to help Stone find this room. Could there be more layers to the intrigue? Stone thought back to all the times his grandfather had read the story to him. The details of the beloved adventure tale came pouring back into his mind: the Amazon, the rainforest, a plateau, primitive people, ape men and....

He smiled. Dinosaurs! As a child, his favorite scene had come toward the end of the novel, when Challenger, to prove the veracity of his claims to the skeptics back in England, released a live pterodactyl, which flew away across the ocean. He'd always asked his grandfather to read that scene at least twice during each reading of the book, and the pterodactyl had become his favorite dinosaur.

"Alex," he called. "Do you see any paintings of pterodactyls?"

"No, only this skeleton," his friend replied.

"Skeleton? Where?" Stone strode to the far end of the room, where Alex stood, inspecting a chemistry experiment in progress.

"Over there, affixed to the wall."

Stone looked where Alex pointed. A replica of a pterodactyl skeleton, at least, he assumed it was a replica, stretched across the wall at the far end of the room. The fabled flying reptile was huge, with a wingspan of more than twenty feet. Stone wondered what it would have been like to see this magnificent creature take wing.

"Is it important?" Alex asked. He sounded disinterested, his attention focused on a vial of golden liquid.

"Perhaps not, but I have a feeling." Stone approached the pterodactyl, or pteranodon if he didn't miss his guess, and looked it over. If it held any secrets, he could see only one possible hiding place. He reached inside the huge beak and felt something thin and solid. Smiling in satisfaction, he withdrew a slender journal book.

"What is it?" Alex hurried forward, his interest in the experiment forgotten.

"My grandfather's journal book." Stone opened it to the back and paged forward until he found the final entry, dated the day before his grandfather had died. The thought caused a lump to form in his throat, and he coughed to clear it away. His moment of melancholy vanished in an instant as the final sentences grabbed his attention.

"*I must get word to Brock. He needs to understand*

*how much depends on him. And he must know that he is
in grave danger."*

7- THE MESSAGE

"You're in grave danger? I suppose you found that out on your own," Alex said. "But what does he mean by *'much depends on'* you?"

"Hopefully, the answer lies here." Stone tapped the journal. "Or in one of the other books."

"You're going to read all of those?" Alex cast a doubtful look at the shelves stuffed with journals.

"If I must, but I suspect this journal is the key. Otherwise, Grandfather wouldn't have hidden it away. I have to warn you, I won't make for good company until I'm finished. I'll need to concentrate on my reading."

"Not to worry." Alex consulted his pocket watch. "I should probably go to work. Will you be here tonight or at your townhouse?"

"Here, most likely."

"I'll see you this evening, then."

Stone bade his friend goodbye, sat down at his grandfather's desk, and laid the book on the table. He closed his eyes and focused on his breathing. As he drew in each breath, he concentrated on the task at hand, and with each exhalation, he expelled all emotions and distractions until his mind was honed to a keen edge. When he was ready, he opened his eyes and started reading.

He'd always been a fast reader with a gift for remembering what he read, but this focus technique, which he'd learned during his travels after leaving the service, made it possible for him to consume and retain great quantities of information in very little time. He finished the journal in less than ten minutes and tossed it on the table, disappointed. He'd uncovered only a few vague allusions to a message Samuel Stone had wanted to share with his grandson, but nothing specific. Undeterred, Stone returned to the shelf, grabbed the oldest journal, and began reading them in chronological order.

Samuel Stone had begun recording his thoughts in his teen years. Though many of the concerns were typical for a young man of sixteen, such as hijinks with friends and dalliances with the daughter of a local farmer, Samuel had also written lengthy, thoughtful reflections on the issues of the day: reconstruction, westward expansion, and the place of freed slaves in American society.

As Stone read, three facets of Samuel's character came to the fore: his love of learning, a desire to travel the world, and an eagerness to go to war. Samuel expressed disappointment that he'd been too young to fight in the Civil War, a regret that eventually motivated him to leave the university and enlist in the army.

Whatever it was about war that captivated Samuel evaporated on the plains of America's western frontier, where the young man witnessed such horrors that he spent the ten years after his stint in the army traveling the world and trying to forget what he'd seen.

As he read, Stone couldn't help but see parallels between his grandfather's experiences and his own. During his decade abroad, Samuel had seen and done much more than Stone had, and he'd fastidiously recorded his experiences. The only exception was the final leg of his ten-year wanderings. The ship carrying him from Madagascar foundered in a storm somewhere in the Atlantic. Samuel had survived, reaching Virginia months later, but though he managed to save his journal book, he wrote nothing about how he had escaped death and made his way home, nor what he did during those missing months. For a man who so exactingly recorded the events of his life, this was a glaring omission.

Stone was closing the last volume when Alex returned.

"You've been at it all day?"

"Just finished." Stone rose and stretched. "What time is it?"

"Six o'clock." Puzzled, Alex looked at the stacks of discarded volumes. "What did you find?"

"He definitely had a message for me."

"And that message was?"

"No idea." Stone was still so focused on the contents of the journals, all the things he'd learned about his grandfather's life rushing through his head, that he felt no annoyance or frustration at his failure.

"You're joking." Alex picked up a journal at random and began flipping through. "He left clues to find the room and the book, but no clues to find the message? That makes no sense." He placed the journal back onto the pile. "Maybe he intended to write the message in the final journal but didn't get the chance to."

"I can't believe that," Stone said. "Whatever the message is, it's clearly important. He would have made sure it was preserved somehow."

"Too bad it's not like that treasure hunt he put together for us on Easter. How old were we? Ten? That was the first time I learned about..." Alex paused in mid-sentence.

"Invisible ink." Stone snatched up the last journal, the one Samuel had hidden in the pterodactyl's beak. "Trinity used to tell me I was the dumbest genius she'd ever met. Perhaps she was right."

He found a candle in a holder on a nearby shelf, lit it, and turned to the back page. He held the paper well above the flame, close enough to warm the page, but not close enough to singe it, and watched as words in tight script appeared.

Brock,

I have every confidence that you will find this letter. You are the cleverest member of my family and the one most like me in character and spirit. You did not tell me why you left after your parents' deaths, but I believe I understand.

We live in a world of wonder, a world of light, but the darkness is ever-encroaching, and it is only by the works of dedicated men that evil can be held at bay. I believe you are such a man. You are gifted in every way a man can be, but you are more than your strength and intelligence. You are a man of character and compassion, and you wield your gifts wisely.

All that I have I have left for you- this house and all the secrets it contains, including a lifetime of knowledge, are yours, but the greatest part of your inheritance awaits you if you have the courage to seek it. You may choose to forfeit it if you wish, but know that I have good reason to believe others will always seek it, sometimes forcefully, and I fear there is nothing you can do to avoid the danger except stand and face it. If you are the man I believe you are, I know you will not turn and run.

If you choose to accept this inheritance, you will have at your disposal the means to stand against evil and emerge victorious. It is my hope that you will do what I lacked the strength of body and force of will to do.

With pride and affection,
Grandfather

Beneath the letter, Samuel had sketched a map of an island chain, the center island rendered in detail, with a dotted line winding around landmarks and terminating at the island's center. The map lacked any names, compass points, or coordinates. Stone would have to match the islands to known maps in order to find his way, and he had a good idea where he should begin.

He handed the journal to Alex and began pacing like a caged puma while his friend read the letter.

"I would ask what you're planning to do about this," Alex said, closing the book, "but I know you too well for there to be any doubt."

"I still have research to do, but when I locate this island, I'm going to find out what's there. Will you go with me?"

"What?" Alex blanched. "I don't… I mean…" He took a deep breath. "I can't just leave work."

"You'll work for me. I'll match your current salary plus ten percent." Stone laid a big hand on his friend's shoulder. "I need someone I can trust, and I don't have anyone else."

Alex looked wildly around the room, as if searching for an excuse. Finally, his shoulders sagged and he nodded. "Of course I'll do it."

Stone felt a flash of guilt. "I know I sprang this on you, and it could be dangerous, so take time to consider before you answer."

Alex shook his head. "No need. I do want to go with you. I've never forgotten the adventures we pretended to have as children. I'd like to experience one real one in my life."

"If you're sure."

"I'm sure." Alex managed a smile. "I'll go with you."

8- THE CHASE

"**Stone!**" **Moses' head** appeared in the doorway. "Miss Trinity called. She needs your help."

Stone didn't wait for an explanation but made a beeline for the doorway. As he took the steps two at a time, Moses followed along behind and elaborated.

"She said she went to the cab company and didn't find nothing, but they acted funny," Moses explained. "When she went to leave, they offered her a ride, but she didn't feel right about it. Now, she thinks somebody's following her, but she ain't rightly sure."

Stone had tasked Trinity with investigating the owners of the cab that had picked up his attacker outside Porter's office. It had seemed a harmless way of diverting her.

"Where is she?" Stone demanded.

"She called from a diner on H Street. She was going to wait for you there, but she thought somebody was watching her, so she decided to walk back to her office."

"Of course she did!" Stone slammed a meaty fist into his open palm. "That's Trinity for you. Impulsive as always. Did she call the police?"

"I asked her that, but she said they'd just figure she was another hysterical woman." Moses forced a half-smile and shrugged, as if to say, *Do you really think I could make Trinity do something she didn't want to do?*

"She's probably right, but I still wish she'd have

called them."

After retrieving his Webley, he ran outside, with Moses trotting along a few steps behind him. He burst through the front door and hurried in the direction of the old carriage house. "You said you've got my Indian running?" he called over his shoulder.

"Yes, sir. It's ready to go."

"Do you want me to go with you?" Alex had appeared on the front step.

Stone shook his head. "You call the police. I don't care what you tell them or how you do it, but get them out looking for Trinity."

Stone's Indian Scout motorcycle waited in the carriage house. Moses had polished it to a high sheen, and the red paint and silver chrome reflected the shafts of afternoon sunlight that streamed through cracks in the wall. The low-slung bike, with its long wheelbase and backswept handlebars, brought back fond memories, but there was no time to reminisce. He hopped on, fired up the engine and, in a flash, was zooming toward the capital city.

Best known for its handling, the Scout wasn't the most powerful motorcycle on the market, but it could hold its own. As Stone accelerated, though, he discovered that Moses had done more than maintain the engine; he'd improved it. He felt a surge of power as the bike hurtled down the road lickety-split. He took the corners as fast as he dared, and opened it up on the straightaways. Before he knew it, the stark, white peak of the Washington Monument came into view.

He performed a few mental calculations. He didn't know exactly where Trinity had been when she made the call, nor what route she'd taken to her office. The most direct path would lead her past the Capitol Building and the Treasury Department. To be safe, he swung around to H Street and followed it down toward the National Mall. Weaving in and out of the light traffic, he kept his eyes peeled as he shot down the street. A few pedestrians cast admiring glances his way— the men at his motorcycle, the ladies at him, but he remained focused on finding Trinity.

The longer he rode without spotting her, the hollower the feeling in his chest. Why had he allowed her to put herself in danger? He'd thought letting her investigate the cab company was a good way to safely redirect her attention, but if her instincts were correct, the company itself was dirty. If anything had happened to her, he vowed to pay them a visit and settle the score however he saw fit.

He slowed for pedestrians at the intersection of H Street and Pennsylvania Avenue and a figure darted out of the crowd, heading directly for him. Unthinking, he grabbed his Webley and leveled it at the figure, who shrieked.

"Stone! It's me, you dolt!"

Stone's entire body sagged with relief as Trinity scrambled onto the back of the oversized seat of his Indian and wrapped her arms around his waist. How many times had they ridden like this in their youth?

"What are you waiting for, you big lug? Go!" she shouted in his ear.

Grinning with relief, Stone took the Indian down Pennsylvania Avenue. As they flashed past the White House, a pleasant wave of nostalgia swept over him. Trinity riding on the back of his bike, barking orders and expecting to be obeyed without question. He'd missed this.

"I knew someone was following me, so I kept ducking in and out of shops and businesses, trying to shake him, but I never could. I was beginning to think you weren't coming. You must have had something better to do."

That was patently unfair. Stone had made excellent time, and if Trinity had wanted immediate help, she should have called the police. But, before he could protest, squealing tires and blaring horns caught his attention. He stole a glance behind him and saw a taxicab bearing down on him.

"It's them!" Trinity shouted.

"I'd like to see them catch us." Accelerating, Stone passed a slow-moving vehicle and then shot across the street. Trinity screamed as they just missed the grill of an oncoming truck, and bounced up onto the sidewalk.

"What's the point of getting away from them if you kill us?" she cried.

Stone ignored her. With lightning-fast reflexes and years of experience, he deftly swerved past a cluster of surprised men and shot back across the road. He took the turn at 15th Street, Trinity leaning into the turn like an old hat, and zipped toward the Mall.

Behind them, the cab came up on two tires as it rounded the corner. Biting back a curse, Stone turned his eyes to the front. It was going to take more than a little fancy riding to escape their pursuers.

That thought had just crossed his mind when a bullet zipped past his shoulder, the hollow report of a pistol scarcely audible over the roar of the engine.

"Now what?" Trinity was surprisingly unfazed by this new development.

Stone began weaving the Indian back and forth. Shooting at someone from a moving vehicle was difficult enough. If your target was moving, it was a nigh-impossible task for all but the finest marksman. Another bullet pinged off the pavement, and then they were crossing B Street, not even slowing for traffic.

"Hold on tight!" He felt Trinity's arms squeeze his waist, and then the Indian flew over the sidewalk and up onto the lawn surrounding the Washington Monument.

"Are they still following us?" he shouted.

"They stayed on 15th. Look out!"

The taxi was running parallel to their course, and the passenger was now braced on the window, taking careful aim. Stone steered the bike up a sharp incline below a sidewalk and the Indian went airborne as shots rang out again. They hit the ground smoothly and he opened the engine up.

"It's no good!" Trinity called. "They'll circle around and head us off."

"I've got a plan." As they closed the remaining gap up to the famed monument, Stone eased up on the accelerator. Surprised pedestrians leapt out of the way, crying out in anger or surprise as the motorcycle zipped past. Bullets still flying all around, Stone circled the monument and made a sharp left. The surprised cab driver stepped on the brakes, the gunman nearly falling from the window as the motorcycle shot across 15th and onto the National Mall.

The Indian fishtailed on the slick grass, but Stone maintained control. As the lush carpet of green flew past, Stone allowed himself to relax, but the moment was short-lived.

"They're behind us again!"

The cab was now barreling down the lawn in hot pursuit. The passenger leaned out the window again and began firing. The shots came at a rapid clip, now, but Stone continued to evade. Soon, the gun fell silent.

"I think he's out of ammunition," Stone said.

"Now we just need to keep them from running us over." Trinity still sounded calm, despite what she'd been through. "Think you can manage it?"

"I've got it covered." Stone eased off the gas, allowing the cab to close the gap between them.

"Shouldn't you be speeding up?"

"Give it a second."

The cab drew close enough for Stone to get a good look at his pursuers. Both were thickset men in suits. The passenger was a greasy-looking character with receding brown hair, while the driver had a square chin, a reddish-blond flat-top haircut, and a scar on his cheek. He gritted his straight, white teeth as he bore down on Stone and Trinity.

When the cab had almost caught up with them, Stone sped the motorcycle up again. He led the taxi on a winding chase along the mall, keeping just ahead of them. Time after time, they crossed over streets that intersected the grassy lawn, but the cab kept pace. Finally, his destination was in sight.

"Trinity!" he shouted. "Whatever you do, don't let go."

"Why would I let go?"

There was no time to answer. Stone cut to the left, slowed a little, and with a jolt they bounded up the steps of the Capitol Building. The cab driver, so focused on running down his quarry that he hadn't realized where they were, hit the brakes hard.

Too late. The screeching cab smashed into the marble steps.

While onlookers rushed to the scene of the accident, Stone skirted the building, coming out on B Street. In front of the Library of Congress, two men in a familiar vehicle flagged them down: Alex and Moses.

"Are you all right?" Alex asked.

"So far, so good. You two take Trinity back to the house. If anyone else is following, I'll lead them away."

Trinity slid down off the motorcycle and gave him a long, searching look. For a moment, he thought she would argue. Instead, she put her hands on his cheeks and kissed him hard.

"Take care of yourself," she whispered.

"Sure thing, dollface."

Stone watched his friends drive away before revving his engine and peeling out. He made several unnecessary turns, all the while checking behind him, but no one followed. The ride gave him an opportunity to clear his head and consider his situation.

Today's events had convinced him that, even if he wanted to forsake his grandfather's bequest, he wouldn't have that choice. Whatever lay on this mysterious island, men would kill to find it, and neither Stone nor those he cared about would be free from danger.

He had to solve the mystery.

9- THE OFFICE

"I can't believe you talked me into this," Alex whispered. He and Stone sat in a greasy spoon just around the corner from the Bermuda Cab Company. The aroma of fried bacon and stale smoke hung heavy in the air.

"I told you, you don't have to come with me." Stone took another sip of weak coffee and pushed his eggs around on his plate.

"And miss out on the fun? Not a chance." Alex consulted his watch. "Midnight. Late enough for you?"

Stone nodded, tossed a few bills on the table, and stood.

"Leaving already, sugar?" The waitress, a curvy blonde in a too-tight uniform, stuck out her lower lip.

"We'll have to drop in again sometime." Alex gave the girl a wink.

Stone thought it unlikely. The food was lousy and, even if he was looking, the waitress wasn't his type. He thanked her and waved to the cook, who nodded to him through a tiny window from the kitchen area, and stepped outside.

"You are something else." Alex shrugged his coat up around his neck and fell into step with Stone.

"What are you talking about?"

"She got one look at you and suddenly her top button stopped working. You can't tell me you didn't notice."

Stone shrugged. He had noticed but wasn't interested. Besides, his attention had been focused on what they were about to do.

"It's Trinity, isn't it? One day back and you're already dizzy with that dame."

"Don't be a twit," Stone said.

Alex only chuckled.

They approached the cab company from an alley. When they reached the back entrance, Stone put a hand on Alex's shoulder.

"Don't bother with the back door." With that, he clambered up the fire escape ladder to the second-floor window. Peering inside, he saw that he had made the right call. It was an office. He scanned the window facing and spotted a metal box in the corner. "It's alarmed."

Alex followed him up the fire escape and moved in for a closer look. After a cursory inspection, he shook his head dismissively.

"Child's play. I clip the right wires and the bell won't ring." He took out a small penknife and cut the wire, grumbling all the while about the lack of a challenge. "Why do they even bother? People should take pride in their work."

Stone slid the window open and slipped inside the office, Alex bringing up the rear. Taking out their penlights, they began searching through the drawers of the large desk that dominated the room. They were breaking the law, but, as far as Stone was concerned, all bets were off since it appeared that the goons at Bermuda Cab had messed with Trinity.

The search turned up nothing of interest— only typical business records and correspondence. Finally, he looked in the "Out" basket on the corner of the desk.

Inside was a single, thick envelope, addressed to a John Kane in New York City. He picked it up and gave it a long look.

"Should we open it?" Alex asked.

"It won't be the first crime I've committed tonight." Stone tore open the envelope and removed the folded papers it contained. He immediately recognized the contents.

"This is a complete transcript of my conversation with my attorney."

"Let me see." Alex examined the paper and a smile spread across his face. "Watch the door. I have an idea."

While Stone waited in the doorway, Alex sat down, took out a fresh sheet of paper, and began to write. When he'd finished, he folded the paper, tucked it back into the envelope, sealed it with rubber cement, and replaced it in the "Out" basket.

"I've always had a knack for copying handwriting," he explained. "When John Kane, whoever he is, receives this letter, he'll have map coordinates guiding to a spectacular treasure your grandfather left you."

"Where do the coordinates lead?"

Alex shrugged. "Somewhere south of Greenland. I just made them up." He made a face. "If he checks them on a map, he'll probably realize they're useless."

"Not necessarily," Stone said. "If this John Kane is searching for the island, he might want to check the location, just to be safe. In any case, it's a good way of letting him know we're on to him, and we won't be intimidated."

Something caught his attention. There was a sound somewhere out in the hallway. He raised a finger to his lips and pressed his ear to the door. He'd always had a keen sense of hearing, and the unique training he'd received had taught him to filter out superfluous noises. Concentrating, he heard the gentle tread of someone trying to be stealthy. The footsteps were approaching the door.

He stepped back and waited, his emotions perfectly calm, but every nerve ending alive. He was coiled to strike.

The doorknob slowly turned, and then the door opened a crack. An armed man, probably the night watchman, peered inside.

Stone struck. In a lightning-fast movement, he slapped the man's gun hand aside and struck the guard with his open palm hard on the temple. His blow was so strong, so precise, that the guard's eyes rolled back in his head, his legs turned to jelly, and he crumpled to the floor.

While Alex straightened the desk, Stone heaved the guard's limp form into the hallway. He took a moment to empty the cylinder of the guard's revolver, pocket the bullets, wipe the weapon clean of prints and replace it in the man's holster. When he'd finished, they exited the office the way they'd come, wiped down the windowsill and alarm, and climbed down the fire escape.

"What's next?" Alex asked as they exited the alley and headed for the corner where he'd parked his car.

"I'm going to ask Trinity to see what she can learn about John Kane. We need to find out who he is and what he wants with us. Perhaps she and her newspaper colleagues can dig up something useful. In the meantime, I'm going to locate my grandfather's island."

10- THE LIBRARY

"Nothing there, either." Stone closed the book and pushed it aside. He stood, stretched, and cracked his knuckles. The popping sound rang out like gunshots in the quiet of the Library of Congress building.

A bespectacled man one table away turned a sour frown in Stone's direction. He opened his mouth to speak, but the words died on his lips as his eyes took in Stone's height and bulk. His cheeks reddening, he cleared his throat and turned back to his own book.

"Sorry," Stone whispered. No need for discourtesy. After all, he was the one making the racket. He sat down again and returned to his pile of books. He'd decided to focus in on the shipwreck that had led to the mysterious time gap in his grandfather's journal. Instinct told him that it was during this period that his grandfather had found the island. Given that he'd kept the place a secret, it stood to reason that he would not have recorded it in his journal.

The ship in question was the *USS Syvarris*. He'd learned plenty about its history, but could find no specific details of its sinking, which seemed shrouded in mystery. Everyone agreed upon the date of the event and that there had been no survivors. Stone grinned. Apparently, his grandfather had never bothered to disabuse anyone of that notion. It was just like Samuel, secretly laughing at the foolish or uninformed. Sighing, he opened another book and flipped through the pages at a rapid clip, devouring every word.

He paused, sensing someone approaching. He knew he was probably safe in the library, but years of training had caused him to keep his senses on high alert most of the time. He tensed and then relaxed as the familiar scent of lilac perfume wafted over him.

"Let me guess," a soft voice whispered in his ear. "You only look at the pictures." Trinity gave his shoulders a squeeze and sat down next to him. "How's it coming?" She kept her voice low and the man at the next table didn't spare them a glance.

Stone grimaced. "It's not coming at all. I'm afraid this was just a trip for biscuits."

"Don't be such a pill," Trinity rebuked. "You'll find something."

"Any luck finding information on John Kane?" Stone asked.

"Not much. He's a rich eccentric. Very secretive. I've asked one of my friends in New York to see what he can dig up, but he didn't sound hopeful." She looked at the stack of books. "What's your status?"

"Can't find the location of the wreck. No specific details in any of these."

"Have you tried newspapers?" Trinity's brow crinkled and the corners of her mouth twitched upward as Stone shook his head. "Your girlfriend is a newspaper reporter and you went for the books first? I'm hurt. Come on." She rose from her seat and strode across the room.

Stone followed in her wake, his head buzzing, but not from thoughts of the shipwreck. "You're still my girlfriend?"

She threw him a withering glance over her shoulder and rolled her eyes. "Yes," she breathed. "Whether you like it or not."

Stone smiled.

Trinity was acquainted with several of the librarians, and her status as a reporter quickly gained them access to the newspaper archives. The way she batted her lashes at the men didn't hurt either. They nearly fell over themselves providing her the assistance she required.

They focused in on newspapers from cities in the Southeastern United States; the logic being that the *Syvarris'* voyage from around the southern tip of Africa would have taken it up the East coast. They chose issues beginning the day of the sinking and up to a week thereafter.

Stone found nothing in the *Atlanta Journal*, but the *Columbia Record* offered a tantalizing clue. The *Syvarris* left San Juan, Puerto Rico the day before the sinking, headed for Charleston, South Carolina.

"Look at this." He showed the article to Trinity. "If we calculate the distance the ship could travel in a day, we should be able to follow its presumed path and get a fair estimate of where it sank. Assuming, of course, it was running at normal speed."

Trinity cupped her chin, pursed her lips, and stared thoughtfully at the newspaper. She was, Stone thought, at her most beautiful when she was thinking hard. It was something about the set of her jaw and the intensity of her gaze that made him sit up and take notice.

"Perhaps," she said after a moment of thought, "but we don't know the exact time of the sinking. A difference of four hours could mean a span of a hundred miles or more."

Momentarily distracted by her lovely face and cute peepers, Stone yanked himself back to the present and nodded. He'd already reached the same conclusion. "Still, it narrows things down a bit. I'm going to dig up some nautical maps of the area."

When he returned with an armful of maps and atlases, Trinity was beaming at him.

"I found another mention of the wreck. A fishing vessel spotted the *Syvarris* about seventy-five miles north of the Turks and Caicos islands. A storm had knocked her off course. Two hours later, that very same ship received a distress call from *Syvarris*. The connection was bad, so they could not get the exact coordinates. The captain headed back toward the spot they'd last seen her, but a storm forced them to turn back before they could locate her."

Stone read the article. Trinity had covered the essentials. He performed a few quick mental calculations.

"Two hundred miles north of Turks and Caicos, another fifty or so north by northwest to the spot where the ship most likely sank." He considered what he knew about that part of the Atlantic. "There are a lot of storms in that area. I know sailors aplenty who avoid it like the plague."

"That bad?"

"If the stories are to be believed, it goes far beyond mere storms. I've heard tell of strange lights in the sky, fogs that spring up out of nowhere, ships becalmed for days, whirlpools, you name it."

"Mermaids and sea monsters?" Trinity's eyes sparkled.

"I don't think you want me to answer that question." He kept his tone level and his expression serious.

Trinity's features sagged. "You're joking."

"Let's stay on task. Here, take a map and search this area." He tapped a spot about two hundred fifty miles east of Freeport. "The island has to be here somewhere."

An hour later, his confidence began to flag. All the maps and charts agreed— this part of the ocean was empty.

"But the island has to be there." Trinity scowled at the pile of maps in front of her as if they had given offense. "Your grandfather survived the sinking. He couldn't have done that if there was no land for him to swim to."

"I agree." Stone rose from his seat. "And I know just who to ask."

II- THE CAPTAIN

"Brock Stone. It's been too long." The corners of Bill Dewitt's eyes crinkled as he shook hands with Stone and Trinity. The years had been kind to the man Stone knew as "Captain." More accurately, Dewitt had looked like an old man for as long as Stone could remember. Decades spent at sea had bleached his thinning hair and thick beard, and baked his skin to a leathery brown. His grip remained strong and he moved with the vigor of a much younger man.

"Good to see you again, Captain."

Dewitt was an old friend of Stone's grandfather and, in years past, had regaled Stone and his friends with tales of the sea. Many were embellished with ghost ships, sea monsters, and mermaids, but they were also sprinkled with the kinds of details that only an experienced sailor could provide. Dewitt had sailed most, if not all of the known world, and served in the United States Navy during the Spanish-American War and the Philippine-American War. The latter conflict had soured him on the Navy so much that he'd retired, bought a fishing boat, and spent the next two decades trawling the waters of Chesapeake Bay.

While Dewitt made coffee, Stone and Trinity admired the contents of his sitting room. Fishing nets that still carried the faint smell of brine hung from the ceilings. Paintings of shipwrecks adorned the walls above bookshelves that brimmed with artifacts of his sailing career, as well as countless old volumes of maritime history, their spines cracked and pages yellowed. According to Dewitt, the furnishings, a simple table and wooden chairs, came from an eighteenth-century pirate ship.

"This is promising," Trinity whispered.

"I should have thought of him right away. I've never met anyone who knows as much about the sea as Captain."

Dewitt entered the room, carrying a tray with coffee in an ornate, china pot, along with three delicate mugs. "I don't keep milk or sugar in the house, so you'll have to drink it black."

That was fine by Stone, who preferred his coffee unadulterated. Trinity managed to hide her distaste for the dark, bitter liquid, taking small sips and smiling politely as Stone and Dewitt spent a few minutes catching up. Stone evaded Dewitt's questions about where he'd been and what he'd been doing the past few years. Instead, he directed the conversation toward the places he'd seen during his time in the Army, of which there were plenty.

Finally, Dewitt set his cup on the table and leaned back in his chair, his expression grave. "I assume this is more than a social call. Don't think I'm not glad to see you, but we haven't exactly stayed in close touch since you went away."

Stone drained his coffee cup and placed it next to Dewitt's. "I'm hoping you can help me. I need to know about the Triangle."

Dewitt laughed. "Oh, I have stories aplenty about that place. Did I ever tell you about the mermaid that tried to drown me? Red hair and the biggest..." He paused when Trinity cleared her throat loudly. "Sorry, young lady. I haven't spent much time in the company of the fairer sex. At least, not the ones willing to spend time with you for free. Of course, there was one girl in Havana." His eyes grew cloudy and he seemed to be seeing something far away.

"Captain?" Stone gently brought the old man back to the present.

"Don't mind me. Just enjoying pleasant memories. Now, which story would you like to hear?"

"We're looking for a place." Stone took out a map on which he'd circled the area where he expected to find his grandfather's island. "It's somewhere in here."

Dewitt's face darkened. "I don't think so." He handed the map back to Stone. "I know the maps of this area well, and none of them show an island in this spot."

"Exactly." Stone fixed him with a level stare. "Which is why I need you to tell me where it is."

Dewitt looked away.

"You know, don't you?" Trinity whispered.

"Captain, did my grandfather ever tell you about the sinking of the *Syvarris*?" Stone asked.

Dewitt stiffened. He rose from his seat and shuffled to the window, the spring gone from his step. "Don't ask this of me, son. You should stay as far away from that place as possible."

"Why?" Stone and Trinity chorused.

"Because you'll never make it to the island alive."

"My grandfather made it there and back again, didn't he?"

Dewitt whirled about to face them. "You have no idea how many good men have lost their lives in that patch of ocean. Thousands, and those are just the ones I know of. That whole place is unnatural. The current is the strongest I've ever seen, and it pulls a ship over razor-sharp coral reefs like a child playing with a toy. The weather's all wrong, too. Lightning shoots out of a cloudless sky. The wind changes direction like a woman changes her hat." This time he didn't apologize to Trinity. "Your grandfather defied the odds. I don't know how he made it onto that island alive, and I certainly don't know how he got away again, but it was a fluke. If you try for that island, you'll die."

Stone nodded slowly. "I understand. But I'm going anyway."

"Didn't you hear a word I said?"

"I heard it all, and I promise you, I've faced worse. Much worse" He rose from his chair and moved closer to Captain. "Grandfather left a message for me. I'm in danger, and will be until I find the island and learn what secrets it hides." He grasped Dewitt's shoulder. "I appreciate your concern, but I'm going no matter what. Either I sail around like a blind fool until I stumble across it or you point me in the right direction. It's up to you."

Dewitt's shoulders sagged. "All right. Your grandfather was the stubbornest man I ever knew, but I think you might have him bested. Give me that map." He took a pen from his writing desk, made a dot on the map, jotted several notes beneath it, and handed it back to Stone.

"So Grandfather didn't tell you what's on the island?"

Dewitt shook his head. "He didn't tell me a thing about the island. He told me about the sinking—how and where it happened. That was enough. I knew it had to be the same island. It's the only one for leagues."

"Thank you. I can't tell you how much I appreciate this." Stone shook hands with the old man.

"Just do me one favor," Dewitt said. "Come back alive."

12- THE TRAIN

The triple arches of Union Station shone dully in the midday sun. The last wisps of morning fog and a whisper of a chill breeze made Alex shiver, but Stone didn't notice. Through study and meditation, he had trained himself to ignore extremes of heat and cold. Now, he feared neither the Sahara nor the Himalayas, though he still preferred a more moderate climate, like that of his native Virginia.

He reached into his coat pocket, withdrew three train tickets, and handed one to Alex and one to Moses.

Moses turned the ticket over in his hand, his lips pursed tightly.

"Is something wrong?" Stone asked. "We're in a nice car, and at very little cost. One of the benefits of the Depression, I suppose."

Moses cleared his throat. "I don't think…"

"Is one of those for me?"

Stone turned to see Trinity, clutching two overstuffed carpet bags, standing a few paces away, smiling.

"What do you think you're doing?" Stone asked.

"I pitched the story of the shipwreck and the lost island to my editor and he loved it! The paper will reimburse me for my travel expenses, but I thought you might be generous enough to pay my way. You do owe me, after all." She winked, her smile transforming into a wicked grin.

"You heard what Captain said; it's too dangerous." Stone looked to Alex and Moses for help, but both had taken a sudden interest in the sky above.

"Save us all some time, Stone. If you don't let me go with you, I'll go alone, and I'll have no one there to protect me. Is that what you want?" Before he could answer, she shoved one of her bags into his arms. "Of course it isn't. Now, be a gentleman and carry my things."

Carrying Trinity's luggage in one hand, his own in the other, Stone led the way into the station.

Designed by famed architect Daniel Burnham, Union Station was a work of art. From the vaulted entryway to the ninety-six foot high, coffered ceiling of the Main Hall, beauty lay all about. Great beams of sunlight shone through spacious windows and skylights, dancing on the polished marbled floor and the gold leaf that decorated the architecture.

"I love this place," Trinity whispered. "It's so pretty."

"Excuse me." A man in uniform stepped in front of them. "Your man will have to use the other entrance."

Stone looked the fellow up and down. He was tall and broad, thin on top, thick around the middle, with the telltale signs of a once muscular frame slowly turning to fat.

"My man? What are you talking about?"

The guard tilted his head toward Moses. "Your man, here. We have a separate entrance and car for them."

It took Stone a moment to realize what the man meant by "them." He dropped the bags and moved closer until he was almost nose-to-nose with the man. "He's my friend and he rides with me."

Color drained from the man's face. He took an involuntary step backward. "I'm sorry, sir. I don't make railroad policy. The other passengers wouldn't, I mean, I'd be fired if I let…"

"It's all right." Moses put his hand on Stone's arm. "That's what I was trying to tell you. Miss Trinity can have my ticket and I'll ride in the other car."

"That's not right," Stone said.

"That's the way it is. I'm used to it. Let's just go before we miss our train."

Reluctantly, Stone relented. He handed Moses a wad of bills, picked up his and Trinity's bags, and headed for the train. Trinity and Alex followed along in silence. A porter took their luggage and directed them to their car on the Southern Railway line. Still fuming, Stone ignored everyone until the train was well on its way. Two hours into the trip, Trinity finally dared speak to him.

"I'm famished. Would you gentlemen care to join me in the dining car?" It wasn't really a question, as evidenced by her standing, taking his hand, and giving it a tug.

Stone allowed Trinity to guide him through their luxurious passenger car and into the dining car. Here, a velvet rope separated the comfortable white dining section from the Spartan colored section. Stone's foul mood returned in full force as he looked at the diners in the colored section gazing despondently into space, hopelessly waiting to be served. Moses sat alone in one of the booths. Their eyes met, and Stone made a small, embarrassed wave, which Moses returned with a nod of his head.

They settled into a comfortable booth and a server, a man clad all in crisp, white cotton, hurried over to them.

"What can I get you?"

"Those people were here before us." Stone indicated the colored section.

The server's face flushed. "We'll get to them shortly."

Stone felt Trinity's hand on his arm and he bit off his retort. He placed his order and lapsed back into frustrated silence.

"You surprise me," Alex said.

"Why? Because I don't like the way my friend is being treated?"

"Because this is the way it's always been, and you're acting surprised by it. Did you forget the way things are in America? Here, in particular?"

Stone considered the question. He had, in fact, forgotten. He'd seen so much of the world, met so many different kinds of people, and been exposed to so many new ideas that his childhood and youth felt almost like a dream. "I guess I did, at that."

Trinity and Alex looked at one another for a long moment. Alex took a deep breath. "Stone, where *have* you been all these years?"

Stone shook his head. "Not now."

"Why won't you tell us?" Trinity sounded every bit the reporter.

"I promise I will. Just not now."

Trinity looked ready to object, but Alex interrupted with a question about how Stone intended to reach the island. They spent their meal discussing the plan in low tones. Afterward, they returned to their car where, drowsy from full stomachs and the hum of the train, they drifted into slumber.

Stone opened his eyes, wide awake in the dark of a moonless night. He heard no sound other than the thrumming of the rail car and the passengers' gentle snores, but he sensed a change. Something had caused him to awaken. What had it been? He turned around slowly, focusing all his senses.

There it was! A slight change in air pressure. The sound of the engine suddenly louder. A rush of cool air. A moving shadow. Someone had opened a window and slipped silently inside. His Webley was stored in his bag in the overhead compartment, but he doubted he had time to retrieve it. Besides, he was unlikely to need it.

He made to rise, but froze when he felt cold steel at his throat.

"Give us the map," a voice whispered, "or die."

13- THE TRAIN AGAIN

Stone moved with the speed of a striking viper. He snatched the assailant's wrist and forced it away before the man could react. Clutching the arm in a vise grip, he yanked the attacker toward him. His fist flew out to meet the man square in the face. He felt the satisfying crunch of the attacker's nose breaking. The man yelped and struggled to get away. Stone grabbed him by the hair, yanked his head down, and drove a knee into his face. He went limp and collapsed to the ground.

It had all happened in a matter of seconds, but the train car was already filled with cries of alarm.

"Stone, what's going on?" Alex shouted. "Are we in danger?"

"Take Trinity and get out of here." Stone opened the overhead compartment and rummaged through his bag. His hands closed on the rucksack in which he'd stored the map and the notes he and Trinity had taken. Hastily, he stuffed them into his shirt and felt around for his Webley.

A boom reverberated through the cabin and the window beside him shattered. Someone had fired at him. In the muzzle flash, he spotted his pistol, snatched it, and hit the ground as another shot rang out. Stone dared not risk pulling the trigger here in the midst of the crowded train car. Instead, he kept low the ground, working his way backward, his weapon at the ready. All around him, people cried out in fear and confusion. Someone trod on his back and fell forward, colliding into another dark figure who shouted in anger and fired a shot into the ceiling as he went down.

Stone reached for the fallen man. His hand closed around the pistol and he yanked it free. The man uttered a confused shout and Stone drove the butt of the pistol toward the sound. He was rewarded with a solid thump as he struck the man on the skull.

Another shot, this time from the far end of the car. The assailants were growing desperate. Stone sprang to the nearest window. Still holding the captured pistol, an Enfield from the feel of it, he struck the window. His powerful blow shattered the glass on the first strike and he ducked as someone fired in his direction.

Not willing to risk hitting innocent passengers, Stone fired twice into the ceiling, hoping to make his attackers hesitate, and then squeezed his bulk out the window and swung up onto the roof.

Clutching a pistol in each hand, he dashed along the top of the car, heading toward the back of the train. The assailants seemed to know exactly what he was doing, because a hail of bullets ripped through center of the roof, shredding the metal and sending bits of shrapnel flying in all directions. Stone had anticipated this and kept to the side, well out of harm's way. He sprinted to the end of the car, leapt over the gap, hit, and rolled to his feet atop the dining car.

"Come and get me," he whispered. Up ahead he saw the lights of Charleston turning the night sky a dull gray.

It didn't provide much visibility, but it was sufficient for him to see the dark shape that clambered up onto the roof of the passenger car.

Stone flattened himself out but held his fire. If he shot the first man he saw, the others might remain down below with the passengers rather than exposing themselves to danger. He couldn't take that chance. He wanted them all out in the open. A second figure appeared, and then a third. They all kept low, and looked all around. They forced his hand when a fourth man appeared from the doorway of the passenger car and climbed up the dining car ladder right in front of him. Stone punched him in the face, sending him tumbling to the ground, but the man's pained cry drew the attention of his comrades who turned and fired as one.

Bullets whizzed past, one taking a bite out of the roof near where Stone lay. He didn't flinch; he'd been under fire before. Instead, he fired off two shots in the direction of the nearest muzzle flash and then rolled to the side as a torrent of bullets buzzed past. This time he saw only two muzzle flares, telling him he'd hit his target. He fired again, two shots with each pistol, each aimed at a different target. In the dim light, he saw both men fall and roll off the moving car.

"Fine shooting," a cold voice said from behind him. "But not wise to leave your back unprotected."

Stone froze. He lay prone, arms extended in front of him. Not a good position.

"Please," the newcomer said, "try and shoot me. I assume you're familiar with the Thompson submachine gun?"

Stone didn't reply. He knew the capabilities of the Tommy Gun, or "Chicago Typewriter" as some called it.

"Make one wrong move and I'll fill you with so much lead we could use you for a boat anchor. Now, toss your weapons over the side and give me the map."

"I'm supposed to believe you'll let me go then?" Stone asked.

"I don't care what you believe. Give me the map."

Two things happened at once. The dining car door below Stone swung open just as the train passed between two steep hills. As the faint city lights disappeared, plunging them into darkness, Stone pitched the Enfield back over his shoulder toward the sound of the voice and rolled off the edge of the train.

As he fell, he caught the lip of the roof with his left hand. He dangled there, holding on with a powerful grip, as the man on the roof, taken briefly surprised when the flying pistol struck him, opened up with his Thompson. As the machine gun sang its deadly song, Stone took careful aim and squeezed off a single shot. The bullet flew true, and the man went down in a heap, his Thompson clattering to the roof and falling uselessly over the edge.

Breathing a sigh of relief, Stone tucked his Webley into his belt and, not a moment too soon, grabbed on with both hands. His fingers and shoulder burned from supporting all of his weight and he took a moment to breathe.

That was a mistake.

He'd forgotten about the open dining car door. As the city lights reappeared, he saw the gleam of a machine gun barrel pointed at him.

"End of the road, crumb. Give me the map or I'll shoot you in the liver," a voice said.

"Shoot me and you lose the map," Stone said. Could

he possibly keep the man talking long enough for a way out to present itself?

"We'll go back for it and your body. It's not a problem. Now…"

The sound of bone on flesh cut off the man's words in mid-sentence. He pitched forward and fell face-first onto the tracks. A familiar form now stood, rubbing his knuckles, in the space the man had occupied.

"Stone," Moses said, "you sure do get yourself into some situations."

14– THE TRIANGLE

"This old bucket doesn't look like much, but she moves along nicely." Alex gazed out at the choppy water of the Atlantic Ocean and smiled. It was a sunny day with calm seas and a gentle breeze. They'd had clear sailing so far, with no sign of pursuit.

"Looks can deceive." Stone maintained a relaxed grip on the wheel as he piloted *Thresher* on a South by Southeast course headed in the direction of the island. Their forty-foot fishing boat wasn't much to look at, to be certain, but she was seaworthy and outfitted with a top-of-the-line engine, plus a few surprises. The remainder of their train trip had gone off without a hitch, and they'd begun what he hoped was the final leg of the journey. His sole regret is they didn't know who had hired the men who had attacked them, though the mysterious John Kane came immediately to mind. "Besides," he continued, "a fancier craft might draw unwanted attention. As it is, we look like just another crew of fishermen trying to scrape a living." He glanced at Alex. "On that note, it's time for you to get up on deck and look busy. Moses is all alone out there."

"You know I sunburn easily," Alex grumbled.

"Next time I'll bring you a bonnet to wear," Trinity jibed.

Alex rolled his eyes before slipping out of the pilothouse and onto the deck, letting in a wave of damp salty air as he went.

"Where, exactly, did you find this ship?" Trinity ran a finger down the pitted glass pane in front of them and frowned.

"I've made a few contacts over the years. This particular friend wouldn't want me to say more than that."

"Not even to me?" She stuck out her lower lip and batted her eyes at Stone. That particular trick hadn't worked since high school and she knew it, yet she kept trying, perhaps for nostalgia's sake.

"Certainly not to a reporter." Stone ignored her frustrated exhalation.

Trinity folded her arms. "When we get home, we need to work on a few of your more annoying habits."

"Such as?"

"Such as the way you keep secrets from your girlfriend. It's getting old."

Stone managed a wry smile. Trinity would keep at him until she got what she wanted, but he planned to make her work for it.

"Don't laugh at me, Brock Stone. I'll…" She lapsed into sudden silence. "It got dark awfully quick, didn't it?"

"I've seen quicker," Stone lied as he scanned the horizon. A bank of low-hanging storm clouds had rolled in faster than he would have thought possible. One moment they'd been sailing under blue skies, the next, clouds of gray. The dim light turned the sea a dark, imposing shade of blue, and a strong wind whipped up whitecaps in their path. The rise and fall of the ship became more pronounced as they crested and descended each swell. "Strange things happen at sea all the time. It's nothing to worry about." No sense in upsetting Trinity with something that was beyond their control. He'd learned many things during his travels, but how to control the weather was not one of them.

Behind them, the door banged open and Moses stuck his head inside.

"Stone, you got to see this."

"I know. The weather took a nasty turn, but we'll be all right."

"It ain't that. They's a ship following us."

Stone snapped his head around. "Following us? Are you certain?"

Moses shrugged. "Sure seems like it. Come out of nowhere and veered in our direction."

"John Kane? The Bermuda Company?" Trinity asked.

"Could be. Moses, do you think you can handle this thing?"

"Sure can."

Moses took the helm, while Stone grabbed a pair of binoculars and strode out onto the deck. He didn't bother telling Trinity to remain inside the pilothouse. He knew she'd come along anyway.

Alex leaned against the stern rail, seemingly oblivious to the fat raindrops that had begun to fall. He pointed a shaky finger at a shadow in the distance.

"It glowed red," he whispered.

"What's that?" Stone put the binoculars to his eyes and focused in on his target. It was a sailing ship, and an old one at that, with shredded sails and torn rigging, but he could tell no more at this distance.

Alex swallowed hard. "I hesitate to say this, but I think it's the *Flying Dutchman*."

Stone lowered the binoculars and gave Alex a

quizzical look. "The legendary ghost pirate ship? Surely you don't believe that."

"It appeared at exactly the same time as the storm." Alex swept his hand in an arc that took in the heavy cloud cover. "And as it turned to follow us, it glowed red. The legends say the same about the *Dutchman*."

"Let me see those." Trinity snatched the binoculars and took a look at the pursuing ship. "I don't see any red lights," she said, "but neither do I see any crew. How could it follow us if it's unmanned?"

"It's the Triangle," Alex whispered. "You know the stories. All sorts of mad things happen here."

Stone shook his head. "You're an educated man. Don't let your imagination run wild. It's obviously a ship that was abandoned and left to drift, and it just happened to come into view as the storm was whipping up. The red glow was probably from a beam of sunlight refracted through a gap in the storm clouds."

"And how did it manage to turn and pursue us?" Alex asked.

"I don't know. Maybe that's just the direction the wind and current are taking it."

He received confirmation a moment later when Moses called out in alarm.

"Stone! I need you in here now!"

He rushed back inside the pilothouse to see Moses hauling at the wheel. The whine of the ship's straining engines filled the small space.

"What is it?"

"Look up ahead."

Stone's eyes searched the sea before them, and then he saw it. They were being drawn slowly, inexorably, into a giant whirlpool.

"Oh my…" Trinity had just arrived inside the pilothouse, and her fair complexion turned pallid as she stared at the spinning, churning water.

"The engines ain't strong enough to get us away," Moses said. "Slow and sure like, it's dragging us down."

"Let me take the wheel." Stone switched places with Moses. "I want you and Alex to raise the sails. I know they're mostly there for show, but we've got a nice tail wind at the moment and we'll need all the momentum we can get."

"You think we can get away from it?" Moses asked.

"Not a chance." Stone set his jaw. "We're going into it."

15– THE VORTEX

"Are you crazy?" Trinity gripped Stone's arm in both hands, digging her fingernails into his flesh. "You're going to get us all killed!"

Stone didn't answer. She wasn't wrong. If his plan didn't work, they were all goners for sure.

"Stone, are you listening to me? We've got to get away from this thing before it takes us down." To her credit, Trinity sounded concerned, alarmed even, but not panicked.

"Find something to hold on to," Stone barked, "and let me concentrate."

Up ahead, the swirling vortex grew larger as *Thresher* bore down on it. Stone didn't try to fight the current too hard. Instead, he kept the boat on a course that would carry them to the edge of the whirlpool. The whine of the engine lowered in pitch to a dull roar as it stopped fighting the greater part of the current and began to move along with it. Stone felt the deck shift under his feet as the craft suddenly gained a measure of speed. Moses and Alex must have unfurled the sails, and now the strong wind was adding its power to that of the engine.

"If you drown us, I swear I'll haunt you for eternity," Trinity muttered.

Stone grinned. Before them, the whirlpool opened up like a giant sea monster's gaping may. Lines of white froth spun down through a funnel of sea green and gray water to a churning pool far below. Stone had looked death in the eye plenty of times, and though it took many forms, it always gave him the same feeling— a heightened awareness of being. Paradoxically, he never felt more alive than when he stood at the precipice of his demise. He sensed everything: every sound, every smell, every texture was suddenly magnified. He was aware of every breath he took, the twitch of every muscle, every bead of sweat that ran down the back of his neck. He felt the surge of the sea through the deck beneath his feet and the wheel in his hands. He smelled the tang of the salty air, the exhaust of the diesel engine, and a hint of Trinity's perfume. Leave it to her to doll up a little even on a trip into the triangle.

Moses and Alex burst into the wheelhouse and froze.

"What are you doing?" Alex asked. "We're about to be sucked in."

"That's the plan." As his friends shouted out warnings, Stone turned the wheel to the port side and guided *Thresher* into the whirlpool.

The effect was instantaneous and alarming. The boat, already shooting forward at a rapid clip, seemed to grow wings as the spinning water swept it in a great, counterclockwise circle. Stone fought to keep them near the edge as they shot forward. "Hold on!" he shouted.

Thresher yawed dangerously to port. Trinity and Moses found handholds, but Alex lost his balance and slammed into the wall.

"I'm all right," he croaked. "Doesn't matter anyway, seeing how as we'll all be dead in a minute."

"That's what you think." Stone gritted his teeth and strained against the wheel as *Thresher* completed its first circuit around the whirlpool. "Just one more time around the mulberry bush," he said.

"How can you tell?" Trinity asked.

"I just can." Indeed, Stone had always had a keen sense of direction that had been sharpened by the training he'd received since he left the service. He kept his focus on the water in front of him, marking the spot where they'd entered the whirlpool in his peripheral vision. His heart raced and sweat now poured in rivulets down his face. Could this work? It had to.

"No no no no no," Alex murmured.

"Everyone say a prayer," Stone said. "Here… we… go!"

He yanked the wheel hard to starboard. The engine whined and, for an instant, he feared it would blow.

"Come on you son of a…"

And then, with a jarring thump, *Thresher* crested the rim of the whirlpool and shot out into open water.

"Thank God," Trinity breathed.

But it wasn't over yet. They had to escape the pull of the deadly vortex. Their spin around the whirlpool had given them an incredible burst of speed, but would it be enough? Everyone fell silent, listening to the roar of the engine as it fought the current. Stone felt the craft begin to slow, and wished he had more to give.

"I suppose we could paddle," Alex offered.

"You're welcome to try." Stone gazed straight ahead, willing the craft to move forward. All around them, the world seemed to slow down as the craft lost momentum to the pull of the water. The whine of the engine grew in pitch.

"It ain't gonna last much longer," Moses warned. "They's limits, you know."

Just as he spoke, the whining dissipated into a low rumble.

"Let me guess," Trinity said. "Out of gas? Threw a rod?"

"Not a chance, dollface," Stone said with a wink. "We're free."

Indeed, *Thresher* now sliced through the waves free and easy. "You two can furl the sails now," he said to Alex and Moses. "We shouldn't need them."

"Nicely done," Alex said. He turned and peered out the pilothouse door. "Looks like we lost the ghost ship, too."

"Think it got sucked in?" Trinity asked.

"I don't know. I'm just glad it's gone."

As Alex and Moses headed out onto the deck, Trinity wrapped her arms around Stone and gave him a squeeze. "That was nicely done. I don't know why I ever doubted you."

"You wouldn't be you if you didn't question my every move," Stone said. "It's what makes you a great reporter. You question everything."

Trinity's gaze softened. "You think I'm a great reporter?"

"Of course I do."

She rose up on her tiptoes and brushed lips against his cheek. "You're not so bad for a big lug. You…" She paused. "Wait a minute. How would you even know if I'm a great reporter? You've been away since before I started working for the *Scribe*."

"I've read your work," Stone said, his brain running a mile a minute to try and recall even one of her articles he'd perused.

"Really?" She arched her eyebrows. "Which one is

your favorite?"

"See what I mean? Always questioning me. You can't even take a compliment."

She put her hands on her hips and frowned. "You're deflecting, Stone. It won't work on me."

"For your information, it was a piece on violence in the Hoovervilles," he guessed wildly. It seemed like the sort of thing Trinity would report on: economic injustice, tragedy, the little guy suffering at the hands of the big lug.

"Oh." The fire in her eyes flickered and died. "Thank you. My editor worried that it was too incendiary, but he ran it anyway. He figured whoever found it offensive would just chalk it up to womanly hysterics."

"You? Hysterical? Never." Keeping one hand on the wheel, Stone pulled her in tightly with his other arm and kissed the top of her head.

She rested her head on his chest and gave a purr of contentment. "I hope it's a romantic island you're taking me to. You owe me."

Up ahead, a fog-shrouded shape appeared on the horizon.

"I think," Stone said, "that we're about to find out."

16- THE REEF

"We'll drop anchor here for now." Stone picked up the binoculars and focused them on the fog-shrouded island. A solitary peak rose up above a halo of low-hanging clouds. Though the distance was not great, he could tell very little about the place. The mist that rose all around rendered visibility almost nil.

"Why so far away?" Trinity asked.

"Coral reefs. Shallow and razor sharp."

"How can you tell they're sharp?"

"Look over there." He handed her the binoculars and pointed to a distant spot to the southeast.

It took her a few seconds to see what Stone had already spotted—a German U-boat, the center of its hull shredded, straddling one of the reefs that guarded the island.

"Odd. It's facing backward, and only the center of the hull is damaged. It's like someone picked it up and dropped it onto the reef." Trinity lowered the binoculars and looked up at him. "How could that happen?"

"A freak wave, I suppose. No telling what the sea will do in these parts." Stone tucked the binoculars into their case and dropped the case into a rucksack. "In any event, I'm not taking *Thresher* across the reefs. It would be suicide."

"How are we going to get there?" she asked. "It's too far to swim."

"Maybe for you." Stone winked. "Don't worry. I have a plan."

Thirty minutes later, they piled into a canvas raft equipped with a powerful outboard motor. Each of them wore a Mae West—the brand new, inflatable life jackets that, when inflated, gave the wearer the appearance of being as well-endowed as the popular actress. Their provisions, along with three Enfield M1917 rifles, were secured in a second, smaller raft tied to the one in which they rode. Stone wore his Webley at his hip, and each of his companions was also equipped with a handgun. He didn't know what they might face on the island and hoped they were sufficiently prepared. Had they carried much more, the rafts would have ridden too low in the water to clear the coral reefs.

He fired up the outboard motor and soon the craft was skimming across the surface of the water. The raft leapt up and splashed down as it crested each swell. Trinity threw back her head and laughed, letting the salt breeze blow back her hair. She always managed to find joy in simple things.

On the other side of the raft, Moses wore his usual, grave expression and Alex's mouth twisted into a sour grimace as he stared balefully at the water.

"Are you nervous or about to be sick?" Stone asked his friend.

"Both. I'll feel better when we're clear of these coral reefs." As he spoke, Alex shot a glance at the reefs that loomed ever closer.

"Worst case, we have to swim for it. You do know how to swim, don't you?"

"Sure. I can swim from one end of the swimming pool to the other. Think that will be enough?" Alex managed a smile.

"If not, you can hitch a ride on one of those sharks." Stone gestured toward the island.

Trinity and Alex immediately scrambled to the front of the raft and scanned the water up ahead. Moses' eyes grew wide and he mouthed, "Lord, save us."

Stone laughed. "I'm only joking. Now sit back down. You're blocking my view."

"Joking, are you?" Trinity looked back over her shoulder. "Then what do you call those?" She and Alex broke apart. Now visible in the gap between them, three gray fins sliced through the relatively calm water behind the second ring of coral.

"I didn't see those." How had Stone missed them? His were the sharpest eyes of the bunch. "It doesn't matter anyway. Those are just sand sharks." That wasn't true, but he didn't want to alarm the others. "They wouldn't dare meddle with us."

The tension drained out of Moses and Trinity, but Alex seemed to know the truth. He arched an eyebrow at Stone, but kept his silence.

"Are you sure we can clear those reefs?" Moses asked.

"As long as I choose the right time. If we ride a swell, we should be fine."

"This had better work." Trinity grabbed her life jacket with both hands and squeezed.

"We're about to find out." Stone gritted his teeth as he gunned the engine and took the raft up onto a high swell. He wasn't worried about his own safety, but he was responsible for the others. He reminded himself that each had come of her or his own volition. The thought was small comfort. Nothing changed the fact that they were here for him, searching for the legacy his grandfather had left him. Not for the first time, he vowed he'd do anything to keep them alive.

"Here it comes!" Trinity shouted.

The raft rose with the water, went airborne, and then splashed down hard.

Moses, his fingers clutching the rope that ran around the top of the raft, managed a grin. "One down."

Stone slowed the raft and cut to port. The sharks still circled up ahead, beyond the next line of reefs, and he saw no harm in giving them their space and crossing a bit farther east. He kept his eyes locked on the coral reef, looking for a break, but he saw none. As they rode along, he realized the surf was now pulling him ever closer to the island and the reefs. Time to pick a spot.

He brought the raft about and aimed for a high swell. He concentrated as the raft climbed the hill of water. Up ahead, the jagged reef rose above the waterline like a sea monster's fangs. Stones's heart lurched. They were going too fast! At this speed, they'd hit the water before they cleared the reef. He let off the engine and felt the craft slow. Alex and Moses both noted the change in the engine's pitch and looked back with twin frowns. Stone gave a quick shake of his head. They could interpret that any way they liked.

He realized he was holding his breath as the raft swept forward and then down with a splash, still afloat. He exhaled with relief.

"That was close."

The ragged sound of tearing fabric, followed by a hard tug on the back of the raft, rendered him mute.

"The raft with our supplies didn't make it across." Moses sprang to Stone's side and began hauling on the rope that held the damaged craft. Stone turned to lend a hand. The load grew heavier as the small raft began to sink. When it was within arm's reach, Moses grabbed hold of the bundled load and heaved.

Just then, the water level dropped as another swell swept toward them. With a cry of alarm, Moses pitched forward and went headfirst into the water.

"Moses!" Stone snatched at the air where his friend had been an instant before, but he was too late. The swell of water lifted the raft and carried it away from the spot where their friend had disappeared. "Alex, take the helm," Stone barked. "I'm going in."

"He's got his life jacket," Alex said. "Just turn around and go back for him."

"I don't see him," Trinity said. "What if his jacket was damaged?"

Stone didn't wait around to debate the issue. His own life jacket would only slow him down and prevent him from diving if need me. He stripped the jacket off, clamped his teeth around the strap to keep it close in case he needed it later, dropped his pistol in the bottom of the raft, kicked off his shoes, and dove into water. Cool twilight enveloped him for a split second, and then he broke the surface and began to swim against the strong current with powerful strokes. He heard the roar of the engine behind him as Alex brought the raft about. He looked all around. Where was Moses?

He reached the spot where he thought Moses had fallen in, and scanned the area. Nothing floated on the surface. Apparently, they'd secured their provisions well, which now seemed to be a negative. The water beneath him was almost opaque. He could see only a few feet below the surface. He'd have to do a blind search.

Releasing his life jacket, he inhaled and exhaled several times in quick succession, then took a deep breath, released it, and dove.

He opened his eyes against the stinging salt water, but he could see little more than dull green and the faint glow of the sun up above. He descended rapidly and hit the sandy bottom after only a few seconds. It couldn't be more than twelve feet deep here. Why hadn't Moses surfaced? Was he tangled in the rope?

Stone felt around for his friend or the sunken raft, but found neither. His lungs began to burn, and he swam hard for the surface. He broke the water in time to hear Trinity call out to him.

"We saw him! He came up for a second and then went back down right over there." She pointed in the direction of the coral reef.

Stone struck out for the spot she indicated, churning through the water with all his might. Up ahead, he saw the top of Moses' dark head bob to the surface and then submerge. Stone dove, grasping with both hands until he caught hold of Moses' arm. He slipped one arm around his friend and swam for the surface. His efforts, added to those of Moses, slowly carried them to the surface.

As the light up above grew stronger, he felt Moses's efforts begin to wane. He was tiring out. Stone kicked harder and they continued to rise, inch by excruciating inch. Would they make it?

And then his lungs filled with sweet air. Two sets of hands reached out and hauled Moses onto the raft. As Alex and Trinity pulled the solidly-built man out of the water, Stone saw that Moses still wore his life jacket and that it was still inflated. Why had he not been able to remain above water?

"Crazy son of a…" Alex muttered.

Stone saw the reason immediately. Moses clutched a backpack in one hand and a sack of provisions in the other. He'd been unwilling to let them go, even if it cost him his life.

"Couldn't…" Moses panted "lose it… all."

"Crazy and brave," Stone said, gripping the side of the raft while he treaded water. "Maybe I should search the bottom and see if I can't bring up any more of our things.

"I doubt you'll find the raft," Alex said as he rolled Moses onto his back. "The current's strong, as you no doubt noticed. He could have drifted a long way from where he recovered the bags."

"True. We're going to be short on provisions and rifles. At least…"

"Look out!"

Trinity's shriek cut him off in mid-sentence, and Stone whirled about to see a gray fin cutting through the water only feet from where he swam.

17- THE ISLAND

Stone's eyes locked on the shark as it surged toward him. The faded gray stripes across its back named it a tiger shark, an aggressive breed responsible for the majority of attacks on humans. This one had to measure sixteen feet—easily the largest Stone had ever seen. He had only an instant to draw the long hunting knife at his hip before the vicious creature was upon him.

In a flash, Stone twisted to his left and struck the shark on the snout with the palm of his hand. The powerful blow served to redirect the shark's attack and push his body farther away from its snapping jaws. Before the shark could react, he drove his knife into the creature just behind its eyes, and yanked himself up onto the shark's back.

The shark immediately began to thrash about, trying to dislodge its unwanted rider. Stone wrapped his legs around the creature's torso and squeezed with all his might. He grasped his knife in both hands and tried to force the blade deeper. The corded muscles of his forearms stood out with the strain as he twisted the blade. Beneath him, the shark's powerful body continued to jerk and writhe. Stone felt himself shift and he squeezed his legs tighter. He'd ridden bulls and bucking broncos out west, but those were child's play compared to this. If the shark managed to dislodge him...

A shot rang out. And then another. The shark

continued to twitch, but the life was draining from its body. All around him, blood filled the water. Alex leaned over the edge of the raft, holding a pistol.

"Get out of there before the blood draws more sharks." He offered a hand and helped Stone into the raft. As soon as Stone was on board, Moses fired up the motor and steered the raft toward the shore.

"Thanks," Stone said. "That was a close one."

"We're not out of the woods yet." Alex pointed to the side of the raft. In its wild efforts to get to Stone, the shark had bitten the raft. The sturdy canvas had held for the most part, but air now leaked from a hand's-length tear in the side. "We've got to get to shore before we sink. And before those things catch up to us."

Stone looked back to see several gray fins honing in on the spot where the tiger shark contorted in its death throes. "Hopefully they'll take a little time to cannibalize their friend before coming our way."

"You're such a comfort, Stone." Trinity grimaced as she stared at the frenzied sharks that now dined on their dead comrade with vigor.

"Hold on," Moses warned. "We're coming up on the last reef."

They plowed through the water, the engine whining as it struggled to drive the now sluggish craft forward. Alex pressed his hands over the rent in the canvas, trying in vain to keep the air inside. The raft was comprised of several separate compartments so a single tear wouldn't deflate the entire craft, but the weight of the riders and cargo was enough that it soon would be swamped.

The last coral reef glistened in the tropical sun, and they bored down on it with agonizing slowness. Up they climbed, the water carrying them forward.

Slowly up.

Slowly down.

And then a hard jolt and a ripping sound. Water began to fill the boat from the stern. They hadn't quite made it across.

"Grab what you can and swim for it!" Stone took hold of the two heaviest bags. He was the strongest swimmer in the group and stood the best chance of making it to shore with their supplies. He waited until his friends were in the water and, buoyed by their life vests, bobbing their way toward shore, before diving in.

The weight of his burden immediately pulled him down, but he kicked furiously, driving himself onward. He'd done more than his share of diving and was capable of holding his breath for long periods of time. Hopefully, it would be enough to get him to the shallows. He kicked with all his might, his sodden clothes and shoes felt like lead weights, conspiring to bear him down to the bottom. His lungs burned and he knew he would soon have to drop one of the bags of supplies and swim up for air. The water around him grew rough, and he felt himself thrown about by the waves rolling toward shore. One of his bags scraped the bottom. Then the other. His foot hit something solid and he pushed upward.

He broke the surface and took a deep breath of blessed air. He kicked furiously, trying to keep his head above water, and his toes dug into the sand. He had made it!

All around him, the others slogging toward shore. Trinity spared a glance for him and smiled just as a breaking wave smacked her on the back and sent her tumbling forward into the frothy surf. She came up spitting and swearing. None of the men dared comment or even crack a smile. Instead, they all pretended not to notice as she brushed her hair out of her face and tried to recover a shred of her dignity. By the time they reached the shore, she was eying them all with suspicion, her eyes daring them to say one word.

Stone looked around. They stood on a sugar-white sand beach that curved off into the distance on either side. A thick tree line of palms, mangroves, and flowering hibiscus and bougainvillea guarded a hilly jungle that rose up to a distant, mist-shrouded peak. He saw no birds, heard no chatter of island life, only the rush of the surf and the whisper of wind in his ear.

"We're alive," Alex finally said.

"But we got no way to get back. I'm sorry." Moses kicked at the sand.

"You got us here safely. That's what matters." Stone looked around at his bedraggled friends. "Let's take stock of our supplies and assess our situation."

They divided up their meager provisions. Collectively, they had enough food for two days if they ate sparingly, plus a single tent, some first aid supplies, a single machete, and a few assorted bits of camping gear. Each person also had a sidearm and a limited amount of spare ammunition.

"It could be much worse," Stone said. "Fresh water is the one thing we're lacking, so keep an eye out for any sources of drinking water."

"You mean like that?" Trinity pointed to the distant peak. Just below the fog, a waterfall poured down a sheer rock face. "It's a long way away, but at least we know there'll be water there."

Stone consulted a copy of his grandfather's map. "It looks like we'll be heading that way. Hopefully, we'll find water before then. In the meantime, it looks like there are coconuts aplenty. I think we should get out of the sun and on the move.

A few minutes later, Stone and Moses were hacking and slashing a path through the thick foliage that barred their way into the jungle. Twenty feet in, however, the growth thinned considerably and the going became easier. They worked their way inward and upward, the hot, humid air leaching the sweat from their bodies. After an hour, Stone called a halt at the foot of a steep incline. They rested in the shade of a calabash tree from which Stone plucked four large gourds. The fruit of the calabash was inedible, but their hard shells could serve as canteens once they found fresh water. Moses and Alex gathered coconuts and they all enjoyed the warm, sweet milk. It dulled the thirst but did not quite sate it.

While the others rested, Stone inspected the hill they were about to climb. It was steep and heavily eroded in places, but he thought they could make it if they stuck to the areas where the foliage was thickest.

"What is that?" Trinity stood and moved to the base of the hill where fallen earth and rock made a loose pile. She kicked at the dirt, revealing something ivory in color and oddly-shaped. "It looks like a bone."

Immediately interested, Alex joined her and began digging. Soon, the two of them had uncovered an elongated skull with deep eye sockets and narrow jaws lined with razor sharp teeth.

Alex brushed it clean and lifted it up for everyone to see. "This," he said in a trembling voice, "is a dinosaur."

"What kind?" Trinity ran a finger along the bony snout.

"I don't know, but it was definitely a predator. Look

at these teeth." Alex's eyes suddenly widened and he wobbled and dropped to one knee.

"Easy there," Moses said. "I know you're excited to find a fossil and all that, but don't fall on your head over it."

Alex turned unseeing eyes in his direction. "I'm not excited; I'm terrified."

Moses and Trinity exchanged puzzled looks, but Stone knew exactly what was bothering his friend.

"That skull," he said, "is no fossil."

18- THE BEASTS

"Let me see that." Stone took the skull from Alex and turned it over in his hands. Sure enough, these bones were not exactly fresh, but neither were they old.

"It's a dinosaur. It has to be a fossil." Trinity's eyes remained glued to the skull. "Doesn't it?"

"These are actual bones. There's even some tissue left on the carcass." Alex said. "When you consider how quickly things decay in a hot, damp environment, these must be fairly new." He picked up a black, curved claw and held it up.

Stone grimaced. The thing looked razor sharp.

"What kind of dinosaur is it?" Trinity bit her lip.

"Velociraptor, I think." Alex handed the claw to Stone and returned to poking around. "They were discovered in Mongolia about eight years ago."

Stone gazed down at the ground as Alex cleared away more dirt and rock. Something bright green and gold caught his eye. "Is that a feather?"

Alex frowned. "It is. And it's attached to a bone. But that doesn't make sense." He picked up the bone, letting the feather dangle. "This bone is light. Perhaps it's hollow like those of birds."

"You can study on that later. What I want to know is, are they dangerous?" Moses turned around slowly as if more of the creatures lurked in the shadows.

"Possibly. They weren't very large— six to seven feet

from snout to tip of the tail and only three feet tall. At least, that's what archaeologists believe." He hefted another bone— this one had three smaller claws attached to what looked like a hand of sorts. "These are what made them dangerous. The talons on the manus, or the hand, plus a larger one on the feet. They could deal out some damage, especially if they attacked in a group."

"The teeth weren't anything to be trifled with either." Stone ran his hand along a line of sharp, serrated teeth set in the skull, perfect for ripping and tearing."

"Y'all keep talking about them in the past tense," Moses said. "But it looks like they're a concern to us right here and now."

"Nothing we can do about it except keep on our toes. Come on. Let's keep on the move." Stone consulted the map and headed off through the jungle.

They soon found themselves on a something akin to a path. Here, the foliage was less dense and some of the native plants had been trampled. It wasn't well-worn, but it made for an easier passage. And it made Stone uneasy.

"I think we need to move into the jungle a bit. I think this is a game trail, and where there's game…"

A rustling in the undergrowth cut him off in midsentence. Trinity screamed and sprang back as a huge, furry creature barreled toward them. Stone had only an instant to register that the four-legged beast was not a bear, as his first instinct told him, but a giant rat. The thing was a good three feet tall at the shoulder and must have weighed four hundred pounds.

Everyone sprang to the side, Stone and Moses leveling pistols at the bizarre creature, but it paid them no mind. It dashed along the game trail, headed in the direction from which Stone and his friends had come. A loud crashing sound came from somewhere up the path.

Stone wasted no time. "Follow me!" He broke from the trail and hurried into the woods, moving quickly and quietly. His companions did the same with varying degrees of success.

"Where are we going?" Trinity said in a hushed voice.

"I'm not sure, but that thing, whatever it is, is being hunted. And anything big enough to hunt it…" Stone left the rest unsaid.

"Was that a capybara?" she asked.

Alex shook his head. "Much too big. I don't know how it's possible, but that's a giant huitas."

"Why isn't it possible?" Trinity frowned.

"They're supposed to be extinct."

The crashing sound drew closer and they all hunched down and looked back in the direction of the game trail. Through the trees, Stone saw a ten foot tall, bipedal creature with stunted arms, a long tail, and a mouthful of sharp teeth. Its hide was light green with muddy brown stripes. A fringe of dark green feathers ran along its spine, down its tail, and along the backs of its arms. As they watched, the creature paused, turned its head from side-to-side, and sniffed the air.

Stone gripped his Webley, wondering if he could do enough damage to this huge beast to bring it down. Far in the distance, the scurrying of the fleeing rat rose above the sound of the wind in the trees. The dinosaur cocked its head to the side, let out a whistle, and took off again.

They breathed a collective sigh of relief and sagged to the ground.

"That was too close." Alex ran a hand through his red hair, which seemed, if possible, to be standing up even straighter than usual.

"Maybe we should get off this island before we get eaten." Trinity glanced at Stone.

"That thing is between us and the beach," Stone said. "Besides, I'm not turning back. If the three of you want to go, I understand, but I don't advise it."

"How *are* we going to get back to the boat?" She asked. "Our raft no longer floats."

"We'll build a new one. In any case, I'm moving ahead. I want to see this through, and I figure I'm as safe in the jungle as I am sitting on the beach. Besides, my grandfather survived this island. I think we can too."

"We should stay together," Moses said. "We can do this."

Trinity and Alex exchanged nervous glances and finally nodded in agreement.

"Good," Stone said. "We'll keep going."

They made their way through the dense foliage, frequently stopping to consult the map and look for landmarks. Thankfully, they saw no further sign of dinosaurs, though Alex jumped at every sound. At long last, they emerged from the jungle onto a ridgeline. A steep gorge ran down to a river far below. Across the way, the high peak they sought loomed against the sky, its waterfall cascading white foam down to the ground far below.

"How do we get across?" Alex folded his arms and looked up and down the gorge.

"We'll find a way," Stone said.

"I think we'd better do it fast. Look." Moses pointed along the ridgeline where, twenty yards away, dozens of snouts protruded from the forest, beady eyes fixed on them.

The creatures began to chirp, the sound rising higher and higher until, in a rush of leaves and feathers, they charged.

19- THE RIVER

"Run!" Stone took aim and squeezed the trigger. The Webley barked and the lead dinosaur dropped in its tracks. He turned and dashed after the others as they ran along the ridgeline. Trinity's eyes were wide and her face a mask of terror. Moses turned and slowed, but Stone waved him on.

"Get them out of here!" He shouted. "There's got to be a way down. Keep running until you find it."

Gritting his teeth, Stone whirled, leveled his Webley, and dropped to one knee. He was gratified to see that several of the dinosaurs had stopped and were now fighting over the remains of the first creature he'd shot. Stone grinned. He was an excellent shot, and three well-placed bullets dropped three more of the small dinosaurs in their tracks. Once again, the flock of vicious creatures descended on their fallen comrades and began to shred their carcasses with ravenous fury.

The predators distracted for a moment, Stone turned and chased after his friends. As he ran along the precarious ledge, keenly aware of the steep drop-off only inches away, he remained alert for the sounds of further danger but he neither heard nor saw anything. That was fine with him.

He broke through the thick tangle of jungle growth and emerged into a small clearing. Here, a single shaft of bright sunlight pierced the veil of jungle greenery. He heard the sound of something heavy approaching from up ahead and saw a shadow moving toward him. He raised his weapon but lowered it immediately as he spotted Moses' sturdy frame emerge from the foliage.

"We found a place just up ahead," Moses panted. "Mister Alex and Miss Trinity are on their way down already. I come to find you."

"I'm fine. Let's get out of here."

Moses turned and headed back into the undergrowth. They fought their way through the jungle's clutching grasp until they came upon what looked like a staircase carved into the stone, descending at a steep angle down into the gorge.

"It's plum strange," Moses said. "They must've been somebody lived here before."

Stone didn't reply. Perhaps there would be time enough later to learn more of the island's history, but right now they needed to get away before the pack of hungry dinosaurs finished their meal.

They negotiated the steps as quickly as they dared. The way was narrow, scarcely wide enough for Stone to remain balanced. What was more, the steps were not perfectly square. Some angled downward, others outward, and the passage of time had eroded many of them, so that Stone and Moses had to choose their footfalls with care.

Alex and Trinity waited at the bottom, twin looks of trepidation marring their faces.

"Where to now?" Trinity asked. Sweat dripped down her face, but she seemed to be holding up well. Alex, by contrast, gasped and rested his hands on his knees.

"I thought you kept fit," Stone kidded his friend.

"Fit… by… city boy standards… I guess," he gasped.

"Well, you'd better catch your breath quickly because I'm not carrying you." Stone ignored the look Alex sent in his direction. He consulted the map. "We need to go east. And that means we have to cross the river."

"It's going to be a rough go," Moses said. "It's fast-moving. I can hear it from here."

Stone craned his neck. Over the sound of the breeze through the trees and the faint cries of dinosaurs fighting over fresh meat far above them, he could make out the roar of white water. "We'll find a way across." He wished he felt as confident as he sounded, but they had no choice. Their destination lay on the other side.

The sight of the river didn't raise his level of optimism. Jagged rocks jutted up through the churning foam, their sharp edges shining like blades in the sunlight.

They gazed in silence for a moment before Trinity voiced the question they were pondering.

"How are we going to get across?"

Stone needed only the briefest of glances to see that his companions were losing faith, and who could blame them? Predators from a forgotten era at their backs and a deadly river in front of them. He needed to act fast before they gave up hope entirely.

"I'll take a rope and swim across."

"Stone, you can't!" Trinity tried to grab his arm, but he was already on the move, and her fingers closed on air. "It's too dangerous," she said. "You'll be killed."

"It's fine. I've crossed worse." That was somewhat true. He'd swum wider rivers, rivers teeming with crocodiles, rivers so frigid he thought he'd die of hypothermia before he made it halfway across, but never one so powerful as this. Nevertheless, he had to try. He dug into one of the packs and pulled out a length of rope sufficient for the task at hand. He lashed one end to the trunk of a nearby tree and wrapped the other end around his waist, securing it in a bowline so it would not cinch up on him should the line go taut.

"I'll swim across and secure the line on the other side. Once I've done that, tie another rope to that tree and use it as a safety line as each of you crosses," he instructed. That way, if someone loses his grip…"

"Or her grip," Trinity added.

"…or hers, you can pull him…or her…back to shore."

"Except for whoever goes last," Trinity pointed out.

"That'll be me," Moses said. "I'm strong and a good swimmer. I can do it."

Alex looked as if he felt obligated to argue, but he hesitated, then nodded his agreement.

"All right," Stone said. "I'll see you all on the other side."

"Wait." Trinity took his face in her hands, raised up on her tiptoes, and kissed him soundly. "That never gets old," she said.

Stone managed a grin. He slipped out of his boots, secured them to his belt, and dove in.

The frigid water sent a shock through his system the moment he touched the surface. The vicious current tore at him, pulling him downstream at a breakneck pace. He let the water carry him—as long as he kept moving forward, he could live with being taken a short way downstream. His powerful legs drove him on and his thickly muscled shoulders fueled the deep, rapid strokes that pulled him through the churning froth. He banged against jagged boulders, sending sharp bursts of pain through his body, but he kept going. The sodden rope and his wet clothing slowed him down but not enough to prevent him from finally making his way, exhausted, to the other side. He scrambled up the bank and secured the rope to a tree.

Stone watched, nerves on edge, as Moses helped Trinity across. His muscles felt like rubber, but he remained tensed, ready to dive in should one of his companions fall, but they all made it, though Alex nearly lost his grip twice during the trek. Stone hauled his bedraggled friend onto dry land, where Alex collapsed in a heap beside Trinity and Moses, both of whom sat catching their breath. He knelt in front of Trinity and laid a hand on her arm.

"Are you all right?"

She gaped at him, eyes wide, but did not reply.

"I think Miss Trinity might be in shock," Moses said.

"No," Trinity managed. "Look!" She pointed a shaky finger toward the sky.

Stone whirled around and bit off a curse. A dark shape swept down toward them. His first instinct was that it was an aeroplane looking to land, but he quickly recognized the long, pointed head, sharp beak, and massive wings.

"A pteranodon!" Alex sprang to his feet, his weariness apparently forgotten.

Stone thought fast. His grandfather's map indicated that a cave lay somewhere on this side of the river. That was their next landmark.

"There should be a cave just up the hill. Let's make a run for it!"

They fled. Razor-sharp leaves on primitive plants

sliced their clothing and sometimes, their skin. Loose rocks turned under their feet, but they kept going. A dark shadow engulfed them and a high pitched, otherworldly cry pierced the air.

Stone stopped running and turned around. The beast's wingspan must have been a good forty feet. Shaking off his shock, he fired his Webley at the creature that seemed to be on top of him. The first shot tore through the membrane of its right wing, and the second took it in the abdomen. The creature's screech turned to a shriek and it wheeled away, not wanting another taste of lead. Stone was tempted to take a few more shots, but why antagonize the beast when he had it on the run? He took one last look at the deadly, yet magnificent, creature before turning to spot his friends farther up the hill. Trinity and Moses stood looking down at him.

"Where's Alex?" he asked.

"He found the cave," Trinity said. "It's just up here."

Stone hurried up to meet them just as Alex emerged from a dark crack in the rock.

"This is the place, all right." He brushed back his damp hair. "And you won't believe what's inside."

20- THE TRIBE

The passageway leading into the cave was formed of smooth stone, as if careful hands had sanded down every rough edge. Behind him, Alex aimed a flashlight into the passageway. Stone felt as if he were entering a temple, but revised this thought when he saw what lay inside.

The walls were lined with bones stacked floor-to-ceiling. And these were no ordinary bones. Carefully, he withdrew from the top of the stack a massive human femur and turned it over in his hands. It was twice the thickness of any he had ever seen and half again the length.

"I'd hate to meet the owner," Alex mused.

"It's not the owner I'd be worried about." Stone hefted the bone like a club. "It's his living descendants that would give me pause."

Trinity ran her hands over one of the piles of bones. "Were these people giants?" she whispered.

"They sure do look like cavemen to me," Moses pointed deeper into the chamber.

Alex turned his flashlight beam at the back wall where an array of skulls leered back at them. Each was impossibly large, with a low, wide cranium, pronounced brow ridge, large nose, and sturdy jaw.

"They look Neanderthal," Stone said. "But they're much too large. Neanderthal were shorter than modern man. These people were huge."

"And the Neanderthal didn't live in this part of the world," Alex added. "At least, not as far as anyone knows."

They continued their inspection of the cave and found a variety of primitive weapons, tools, and seashell jewelry lying in a deep pit at the center of the main gallery, which lay only a short distance from the cave mouth. The place had a ritualistic feel about it. Had they intruded on the religious center of an extinct tribe of hominids?

"Is it possible that Neanderthals could have lived here?" Trinity scooped up a handful of shell necklaces and let them spill back into the pit.

"Considering we've discovered living dinosaurs on this island, I'd say it's not beyond the realm of possibilities that some larger cousins lived here." Stone replaced the femur and moved deeper into the cave.

"You mean *live* here," Moses corrected.

"What's that?" Stone turned and his instincts immediately went on full alert at the sight of his friend's wide eyes and trembling hands.

Moses shivered and inclined his head toward the cave mouth. Down the hill, dark shapes gathered at the river.

Stone's mouth went dry. Even at this distance, he could see them clearly—they were, indeed, giant, primitive humans. His sharp eyes passed back and forth across the gathered throng, taking in every detail. The largest stood a good seven feet tall with impossibly broad shoulders and powerful muscles. They were armed with a variety of weapons: heavy wooden clubs studded with shark's teeth, spears tipped with stone points, slings, and long, sharp teeth that must have belonged to dinosaurs at one time, which they wore tucked into their simple hide belts like knives. Each wore simple armor made of hide and bones.

One man, the largest of the lot, gestured and moved his lips. Clearly, these primitives had developed some form of speech. This revelation sent a chill down Stone's spine. The numbers and apparent physical prowess of these new arrivals presented enough of a challenge, but if they were intelligent enough to form a battle plan, they posed an even greater threat. Just as the thought passed through his mind, the cavemen, as he found himself thinking of them, fanned out and began making their way up the hill. There were at least forty of them, and they all knew how to use the terrain to their advantage, keeping low and using every available tree and boulder for cover.

"It's almost like they've been exposed to gunfire before," Stone whispered.

"They have slings, so they're no strangers to projectile weapons," Alex noted.

"They surely must know how to hunt," Moses said, "and protect themselves from the dinosaurs." He looked at Stone. "Can we stop them?"

"I don't know." Stone hated to admit it, but it was the truth. "We'll have to make every bullet count and hope our weapons pack enough punch to penetrate their armor and thick bones. And even if we succeed, we'd probably exhaust our supply of ammunition in the process, leaving us nothing for whatever lies ahead."

"Then we run?" Moses sounded doubtful

"No good. The only way out is through their line." Stone took a deep breath. "The map indicated that we had to pass through this cave in order to reach our destination. We just need to find the way out."

"That could be a problem," Alex sad. "I've been all around this chamber and there's no other passageway leading out. Not anywhere."

"There has to be." Stone fingered his Webley. "You and Trinity keep looking. Moses and I will get ready for a fight."

21- THE ESCAPE

Stone watched the line of cavemen as it moved ever closer. Would they flee if he took out a few of them? He supposed they'd find out soon enough.

"I don't suppose they'd let us go if we asked them nice?" Moses asked.

"You're welcome to try, but even if they speak English, I don't think they'll forgive us for invading their sacred burial chamber, assuming, of course, that's what this is." Stone stole a glance back into the cave. "Any luck?"

"No," Alex replied. "I don't know where you expect us to look. We've checked everywhere, except…"

Stone suddenly remembered an odd, dotted line on his grandfather's map. A line that ran downward from the cave and then back up again. Almost as if it denoted an underground tunnel. "Except in the bone pit." A sudden conviction filled Stone. "Pull all the bones out of the pit. Hurry!"

"Are you serious?" Trinity protested. "That's disgusting, Stone! It's like, robbing a grave."

"It has to be done. Now hop to it!" Stone and Moses exchanged rueful grins.

"We're going to need some time," Alex said. "This thing is pretty deep."

"I'll see what I can do to slow them down." Stone turned to Moses. "Cover me."

Moses' eyes bugged out. "What are you fixing to do?" He looked out at the approaching throng of cavemen and then back at Stone.

"I'm going to ask them nicely." He holstered his Webley, took a deep breath, and stepped out into the sun.

As he'd hoped, the cavemen slowed their advance. The largest man and ostensible leader raised a beefy hand and the line halted. They stood there, humid air and silence hanging between them until Stone spoke up.

"We're sorry we entered your cave. We didn't know it was sacred."

The cavemen stared blankly at him. Stone hadn't expected to be understood, but that wasn't his goal.

"If it's all right with you, we'll just walk away." He held one hand flat and, with two fingers of the other hand, mimed walking, then pointed off into the distance. A few of the cavemen chuckled. At least, he thought the guttural sound paired with bared teeth was laughter.

"There *is* something down here!" Alex called from inside the cave. "I see a handhold."

At the sound of Alex's voice, the lead caveman started forward.

"Wait a minute!" Stone held his hands palms outward. "We can talk about this. There is no need for anyone to get hurt. All we want is to leave in peace."

He saw a flicker of movement out of the corner of his eye and ducked as a rock, most likely hurled from a sling, whistled past his head and smashed into the rock wall behind him. With a resounding roar, the cavemen charged.

A shot rang out and the lead cavemen went down, clutching his chest. Moses had chosen his target carefully, but it made no difference. The rest of the attackers paid no mind to their fallen compatriot.

"Back into the cave," Stone ordered. "The narrow entry will choke them off and make it easier to defend. We'll clog it with their corpses if we have to."

But they didn't have to make a fight of it; at least, not yet. Inside, Alex and Trinity had reached the bottom of the bone pit and were heaving at a round plug set in the floor. Stone dropped down beside them, slipped his fingers into the handhold, and heaved. The plug resisted for a moment, then popped free like a cork from a champagne bottle. Stale air wafted upward. "Inside. Now!"

Thankfully, Trinity neither protested nor asked for an explanation, but plunged into the hole. Alex followed.

"Moses! Get down here!"

The pistol cracked again, and then Moses' beefy form hit the floor. "I got two of our supply packs," he huffed.

"Good." Stone took one of the packs from his friend. "Now let's scoot."

They dropped into the pit, which proved to be only about seven feet deep. Stone took a moment to replace the plug before looking around. A narrow passageway angled downward, and Alex, flashlight in hand, was already moving ahead.

"You think they'll follow us?" Moses stared up at the now-closed entryway.

"If they do, they'll have to come single-file. I'll gladly take my chances in that scenario. One or two of those big fellows' corpses will block the way nicely."

The passageway only descended for a short distance, and then it began to climb again at a steep angle, just like the map indicated. Occasionally, they were forced to stop and clear away rubble that had fallen from the ceiling. Stone privately wondered what they would do should they come to an impassable section. Go back and fight their way out, he supposed.

After an hour, they came to a small chamber where the floor was relatively level, so they stopped to rest. Moses passed around dried beef and a canteen.

"What do you think we're going to find on the other end?" Trinity asked.

"I wish I had a guess." Stone rose to his feet, stretched, and circled the cavern. Alex's flashlight cast deep shadows on the walls, and something caught Stone's attention. "Alex, turn your light this way." His friend complied, and the beam illuminated two words carved in the rock.

SAMUEL STONE

Stone's mouth went dry. "My grandfather was here."

This proclamation energized his friends. They huddled around him to see the place where Samuel Stone had carved his name decades before, and then they searched the cavern for more markings, but found none. Finally, they decided to move along.

"Whatever we're headed toward," Trinity said, "must be what your grandfather wanted us to find. And it must not be too dangerous since he lived to tell about it."

"He lived, but he didn't tell," Stone corrected. "That's why we're here."

"I still don't understand," Trinity said. "If it's so important that you find this place, why did he keep it a secret?"

"He probably wanted to wait until he thought I was old enough. But then I… disappeared." He felt three pairs of eyes on him, but no one asked the question he'd constantly declined to answer. When he was ready, he'd explain himself. But not now.

"I see sunlight up ahead," Alex called.

Stone drew his Webley and moved to the fore. He rounded a corner into bright sunlight and froze.

"I don't believe it."

22- THE VALLEY

Below them, nestled in a small valley, lay a city like none Stone had ever seen. A stone pyramid, smooth-sided in the Egyptian style, stood at the center. Despite the cloud cover that blanketed the sky, the pyramid's gold-flecked stone surface seemed to sparkle. A series of perfectly straight roadways of gleaming white sand radiated out from the pyramid like the spokes of a wheel. Neat stone houses, tiny gardens and orchards, and small greenways filled the spaces in between. Slender, dark-skinned people went about their normal activities, seeming oblivious to the intruders into their domain. Everything appeared calm and orderly. It was amazing.

"What is this place?" Trinity marveled, gazing down at the scene with eyes filled with wonder. "I have never seen its like."

"It is called Ogygia," a mellifluous voice said from behind them.

Stone whirled about. His Webley was in his hand and trained on the figure behind them in a flash.

A thin man with glossy black hair and skin the color of coffee with cream raised his hands, palms outward, and smiled. "Please put down your weapon. You are safe here." He looked on placidly as Stone holstered his pistol. "My name is Malik. I bear you no ill will."

"I'm Brock. This is Trinity, Alex, and Moses." Eyes still on the newcomer, Stone inclined his head toward each of his companions as he named them.

Malik bobbed his head at each person as Stone introduced them.

"How did you know we were here?" Stone asked.

"We watch," the man said simply. He pursed his lips and pointed with them, in the fashion Stone had seen among peoples in other parts of the world, back in the direction from which they had come. Two figures, one male, one female, melted out of the jungle. Each carried a spear and wore a knife at the belt and a bow and quiver across the back. "The Varri seldom try to invade our valley, but it has been known to happen. This is one of the possible paths by which they could enter."

"How is it that you speak such good English?" Trinity edged closer to Stone as the armed warriors moved closer.

"You are not the first outsiders to come to Ogygia. We learn all we can from them." He paused, looking expectantly at each of them in turn. "Perhaps you can tell me how you came to us."

"Dinosaurs and cavemen chased us," Alex said. "The ones you call the Varri."

"But how did you come to be on the island in the first place?" Malik pressed.

The others cast nervous glances at Stone, but he replied easily. "We sought the island out. It wasn't easy, but we found it."

Malik's eyes narrowed. "That is… unusual. People come to us one of two ways: by shipwreck or by losing their way. Why would you seek us out?"

Stone took a deep breath. "I think I was supposed to come here. At least, someone wanted me to."

Malik tilted his head, a look of curiosity in his eyes,

but he did not interrupt.

"My grandfather left me a message urging me to find this place. And he left a map."

"Where did he get such a map?"

"He drew it. I think he was once a castaway here among you."

Malik's dark gaze grew flinty. "Few have left the island, and the chances of escaping alive are slim. What was his name?"

"Samuel Stone."

The reactions to that name were immediate. Malik flinched and the warriors muttered something inaudible. Malik silenced them with a sharp, cutting gesture.

"In that case," Malik said, "you must come with us."

He led them in silence down a winding path into the lush valley. Stone had many questions he wanted to ask. Who were these people? Who were the Varri? How did they keep the dinosaurs at bay, or did they? And, if very few outsiders left the island, what happened to the rest of them? He didn't bother asking; the expression on Malik's face told him no answers would be forthcoming.

When they reached the city, Malik led them past gawking onlookers toward the pyramid. Among the natives, Stone noticed many light-colored eyes and some people with skin several shades lighter than Malik's. That answered his question about outsiders. Clearly, they had been assimilated into the community here. Perhaps that boded well for him and his companions, but it didn't necessarily mean that those people had stayed here of their own free will.

"Are we in danger?" a soft voice whispered. Trinity had edged up alongside him and now looked at him with concern brimming in her brown eyes.

Stone shrugged. They were outnumbered and outgunned, despite the natives' primitive weapons, but Malik hadn't disarmed him or his companions. Surely if he meant them ill, he would have deprived them of their best means of defending themselves. "We're okay so far," he finally said. "Don't worry. I'll get you out of this." He forced himself to meet her gaze, willing her to believe that of which he was not quite certain himself.

When they reached the pyramid, he was surprised when Malik did not lead them down into its depths, but instead turned right and ushered them into a walled garden. Here, among a grove of orange trees, a tall, broad-shouldered man stood waiting.

Like some of the others Stone had seen, this man had grey eyes and skin only a few shades darker than his own, though his black hair and wide nose and forehead gave testament to the native part of his ancestry.

Malik gave this man the same bob of the head he'd made when meeting Stone's companions. "Akente," he began, "these people have come here…" He paused. "They say they were sent here by Samuel Stone."

Akente did a double-take, then smiled and approached them. Unlike most men Stone encountered, Akente was almost his equal in size. When the man offered his hand to shake, Stone felt his powerful grip and knew he would be a dangerous adversary.

"I am Akente." His smile was friendly, but his eyes told a different story, though Stone couldn't be sure what that was. Suspicion? Amusement, even?

"I am Brock Stone."

"Ah, I knew you were a Stone the moment I laid eyes on you," Akente said.

"How could you know that?" Trinity asked.

Now, Akente's smile finally reached his eyes. "Because I am his uncle."

23- THE

REVELATION

"My uncle?" Stone didn't need Akente's nod of the head to know it was true. Clearly, his grandfather had sired a son while on the island.

"Just so," Akente said. "My mother was immediately taken with this exotic stranger, and though he remained with us only a short time, it was time enough."

"Did he marry her?" Trinity's cheeks flushed a rosy pink and she stole an unreadable glance in Stone's direction.

Akente laughed. "I am afraid that when it comes to choosing a mate, we do not share your society's institutions, nor your peculiar reservations about what is, to our minds, a very natural act."

Trinity's face burned scarlet, while Alex and Moses turned away before she spotted their smiles.

"Can you tell me anything about the time my grandfather, your father, spent here?" Stone asked.

Akente wiggled his elbow in what Stone took to be equivalent to a shrug. "A little bit. But my mother can tell you more."

"She's alive?" No sooner had the words passed her lips than Trinity brought her hand to her mouth. "I am so sorry. I only meant, since Stone's grandfather is dead…"

"I understand," Akente said, smiling graciously. "My mother was young, barely a woman, when my father came here. She is old now, of course, but she still has her mind and her spirit. I will take you to see her if you wish."

"Please," Stone said.

Akente led them out of the garden and out toward the outskirts of the city. As they walked, Moses fell into step with Stone.

"You *sure* this ain't a trap?" he whispered.

"I'm sure it doesn't matter," Stone replied. "If it comes to a fight, we're in bad shape."

Moses nodded, clearly unsatisfied with the answer.

Akente halted at a low stone building. "This is my home. Wait here, please." He disappeared through an arched doorway, returning moments later. "Please come inside. We have food and drink for you." He made a slight bow and swept his arm toward the doorway like a maître d' showing guests to their table.

The flat-roofed house consisted of one large room. Sunlight shone in through open windows all around. Stone noted there were no windowpanes, only thick curtains woven of some tough fiber, drawn back to let in the light. The walls were coated in a stucco-like substance and painted in brightly-colored murals depicting scenes from nature. A sunrise decorated the East wall and a sunset the West, while the north wall was a starry night and the south a stormy sky. Woven blankets lay on the stone floor, encircling a crackling fire. Beyond, covered in a fur blanket, a dark-skinned, silver-haired woman reclined against a pile of cushions.

"You are welcome here." Her strong voice resonated

through the chamber. She gestured with a leathery hand toward the blankets and Stone and his friends lay their packs down and took seats on the blankets. "I understand you are Samuel Stone's grandson," she said as soon as Stone's backside hit the floor.

"Yes ma'am," he replied.

Her sharp eyes narrowed. "What is that word?"

"Sorry," Stone began, "where I grew up, it is a term of respect for an adult woman."

She considered this for a moment. "In Ogygia, we are known as we are known. You will call me Talisa. Now, tell me why you have come here and why you brought weapons with you."

"We brought the weapons because we did not know what dangers we might encounter," Stone said.

"A good thing, too, considering we met dinosaurs along the way," Alex interrupted.

The woman frowned and glanced at Akente.

"The *stelli*," he said.

"Speaking of them dinosaurs," Moses said, "how come they don't come after you? The flying ones, I mean."

"The pyramid keeps them away," Talisa said.

"How does that work, exactly?" Alex asked.

"We do not know. The knowledge came to us from lost travelers many summers ago, but they did not pass the knowledge down to us."

"The stelli do not approach our valley any longer," Akente said. "Save for the occasional youngling, and they turn and flee when they come too close."

"Have any ever broken through?" Stone asked.

"Rarely. And they die in the attempt." Akente smiled.

"Does the pyramid keep the Varri away as well?" Trinity asked.

"No," Talisa said simply.

"The Varri are human." Stone said. "I imagine any power that would drive them away would have the same effect on the people of Ogygia."

"You have not told me why you have come here." Talisa's voice cracked like a whip.

Stone sat up straight, like a reprimanded schoolboy. "My grandfather wanted me to come here. He left me a map and a message that I must find the island or I would be in danger." Stone paused. "I can't say for certain what that danger is, though men have been trying to kill me ever since his death. I can only assume that someone found out about his time on the island and wants whatever he discovered here."

Talisa remained silent, but Stone noticed that she no longer looked him in the eye.

"Can you help me? Do you know what he discovered while he was here? What could make it worth me endangering my life to make this trek? And why are men trying to kill me?"

Talisa gazed at the fire. "I do not know what he discovered."

Stone's spirits fell at her pronouncement but lifted at her next words.

"But I know where he found it." She looked at him with a sad smile. "Samuel spent his days exploring as much of the island as he dared. And he spent his nights with me," she added with a grin that made Trinity shift uncomfortably. "The night before he left, he told me of a cave he discovered. He called it a…" She frowned and pressed her fingers to her temples. "What is your word?

Revolt? No. A revelation. He said what he found there could change the world…or destroy it."

"Can you direct me to this cave?" Stone felt like springing to his feet and dashing out the door in search of this cave, but he waited.

"It is dangerous. You must climb the volcano and find the passageway that descends into its depths."

"I can do it," Stone said.

A commotion arose from outside the house and Akente hurried to the doorway. Angry voices speaking in an unfamiliar language echoed through the house.

Talisa listened for a minute, then inclined her head. "It is Samman, a member of the council. He knows that a group has arrived, among them a man claiming to be Samuel's descendant. He is angry that Akente did not present you to the council immediately as we are expected to do with all new visitors."

"Are we in danger?" Trinity asked.

Talisa made the same elbow-wagging motion they had seen Akente make earlier. "Visitors are always brought into our society, provided they do no harm. But they will watch you closely." She frowned and lowered her voice. "They cannot know about the cave. Samuel made that clear."

Stone rose just high enough to peer through the window. Samman was a powerfully-built man with bronze skin and black, curly hair. He was flanked by half a dozen men— some armed with bows, and two with old flintlock muskets, probably the spoils of an old shipwreck.

"I don't see any way around this," he said to his companions, "outside of grabbing our guns and attacking them, but that is unwarranted. They only want us to meet this council."

"But what if they don't allow you to search for the cave?" Trinity asked.

Alex rose to his feet. "Go and find your cave," he said. "We'll be here when you get back." Before Stone could reply, Alex tossed him one of the backpacks. "Quick. Out the window before they encircle the house."

"Do it," Trinity whispered. "Like Talisa said, we're safe provided we do no harm."

"I can't leave you."

"We done went through too much for you to give up when you're almost there," Moses said.

"But they know I'm here," Stone protested.

Alex smiled. "Correction. They know a descendant of Samuel Stone is here." With that, he turned and strode out the door with his hands upraised. "I am Alex English," he bellowed. "I am Samuel's grandson."

"There's nothing for it now." Trinity managed a grin. "If you go out there now, they'll know him to be a liar and then we're all in trouble." She took Stone's hand and gave it a squeeze. "Get out of here."

Stone saw the wisdom in her words, though every fiber of his being told him to stay and fight. Mouthing a word of thanks to Talisa, he reluctantly moved to the rear window and sprang through. When he hit the ground, he began running at full tilt toward the volcano, and whatever secret lay within its depths.

24- THE TRAITOR

Samman raised his arms, palms open and turned outward, above his head, and crossed his wrists. The burly Varri guard who blocked his path stared daggers at him before finally lowering his spear and motioning him forward. Samman brought his hands down but kept them visible. He could retrieve any of his three hidden knives and hurl one into the brute's eye in a flash should the need arise.

"I talk to Krell," he said simply. The Varri favored a simple vocabulary to go along with their limited imaginations, so the fewer words one used when speaking to them, the better.

The hulking figure nodded and indicated that Samman should lead the way. Just his ill-fortune that he would stumble across one of the least idiotic of this primitive tribe. He was keenly aware of the spear point that hovered just inches from his back. He felt fairly certain he could still kill the Varri if he had to, but it would be a close thing and he might suffer injury in the process. No need for that if it could be helped.

Samman picked his way along the well-worn path that led to the cliff dwellings where the Varri made their homes. All around him, he heard the buzzing of insects and the distant cries of more sinister creatures. They passed through a sunlit clearing and he glanced up at the sky. High above, he saw the shadow of a predator on the wing and he keenly felt the absence of the protection the pyramid afforded his people. Perhaps he was still close enough for some of its power to still be felt because the creature continued to soar along, paying him and his escort no mind.

They arrived at the Varri home in short order. Here, the jungle had been cleared away from a sheer cliff face of yellow stone. Caves shaped and expanded by human hands pitted the surface, if the Varri were, in fact, human. That particular issue had been the subject of much debate in the Ogygian council. Rough staircases wended their way up and down the cliff, and Varri of all ages milled about. A few of the primitives gazed at him with dull eyes that conveyed a touch of curiosity, but most looked away as soon as they spotted his approach. He was no stranger to this community and thus not much of a curiosity to the Varri, though his visits here were unknown to the people of Ogygia.

When he reached the mouth of Krell's cave, he stopped just outside and waited to be acknowledged. Krell spotted him immediately, of course, but pretended to be unaware of Samman's presence until what he considered to be a suitable time had passed. Finally, he invited Samman in with a single word.

"Come."

A smoky fire warmed the cool, damp cave. Krell sat beside it on a thick fur, sharpening a stone knife. Samman knew the primitive's attention span was brief, so he began speaking the moment he reached the circle of firelight.

"I need your help."

Krell tilted his head to the side and stared at Samman.

"Intruders in my home. My people let them stay. Intruders must be killed."

Krell tilted his head farther until it rested on his shoulder, his gaze flat. His countenance conveyed a single question: Why should I care?

"My people must be punished," Samman said. A spark of interest flared in Krell's eyes, and Samman knew he had the brute's interest. "I know you want food and women. If you do this, you may take them from our valley one time." He held up a single finger.

Krell climbed to his feet, muscle and sinew rippling in the firelight. He walked around the fire and stopped when he stood almost nose to nose with Samman. His breath smelled of the sour leaves the Varri loved to chew.

"Intruders already fight us. Kill."

Samman nodded. "You can get your revenge."

"How do we do this?"

Samman's spirits leapt. It was going to work! He opened his mouth and then closed it almost immediately, biting off the words before he uttered them. A flicker of self-doubt sparked in his mind as he imagined the toll this decision would make on his people, but he had no choice. For too long he had counseled against allowing outsiders into Ogygia. His people must experience the consequences of relaxing their vigilance firsthand. A Varri raiding party springing up in the middle of their valley would achieve just that. By doing this, he might finally convince them to completely seal themselves off from the rest of the world. What's more, the raid would provide the perfect cover for him to kill the outsiders whom the council insisted on coddling. It had to be done.

He swallowed hard and spoke the words.

"I will let you in."

25- THE CAVE

Stone worked his way up the steep, rocky slope. He hated leaving the others behind, but he knew this would likely be his best chance to solve his grandfather's mystery. No telling what the council might decide. Better to take action now rather than wait upon the unknown.

Loose rocks shifted beneath his feet, causing him to slide, but he continued his ascent. His muscles strained as gravity's clutching hands fought to hold him back. As the way grew even steeper, he was forced to find handholds in the volcanic rock, and he moved along in a half-crawl. Somewhere in the distance he heard the keening cry of what he hoped was a bird of prey. More likely, it was a pterodactyl. He hoped Talisa was right about the pyramid keeping the dinosaurs, or the stelli as she called them, at bay.

Humidity and his own perspiration quickly soaked through the fabric of his clothing. The exertion felt good. He hadn't realized how much he missed climbing. Before he knew it, he'd reached the top of the volcano.

Gazing through the haze of volcanic gases wafting up from the crater, he scanned the dark rock, looking for any sign of a cave. Not for the first time, he wished his grandfather had left more explicit instructions.

Cracks in the rock, many cast in deep shadow, lay all about. Any one of them could hide the entrance. It would take forever to search them all. He needed to find a way to narrow things down.

He sat down on a nearby rock, allowed his eyes to slide out of focus, and began the breathing technique he'd learned in the Far East. In and out, focusing all his awareness, bringing all his senses and mental acuity to bear.

When his eyes snapped open, he once again scanned the inside of the volcanic cone, this time with machine-like precision. His eyes took in every detail, his brain processing the information in a flash. In moments, he had discarded entire sections of the cone as unlikely spots for a cave due to the steepness of the sides, the thinness of the cracks, or the emission patterns of the gases that poured forth from beneath the earth.

He quickly identified the most likely spot into which his grandfather would have descended. He concentrated on it, and his sharp eyes picked out, not a path, but a line in which the angle of the slope was a little less steep. It was so subtle he had overlooked it the first time, but now it seemed to shine as his eyes locked on it.

He made his way down to the spot he'd seen, where he found a narrow crevasse that cut at a sharp angle down into the volcanic rock. Not sure if it would prove to be a dead end, he squeezed his bulk into the narrow space and began working his way down into the darkness. The confining quarters constricted his chest and restricted his breathing. A less-experienced man might quickly succumb to claustrophobia and panic, but this was hardly Stone's first caving experience and he knew that any spot he could get into, he would be able to get himself out of again.

He pressed on, sometimes having to force the air from his lungs in order to negotiate a particularly narrow spot, but finally the way opened up enough for him to move easily and, more important, breathe freely. A few more minutes of feeling his way in the dark and he was able to walk normally. With room to now get into his rucksack, he retrieved his flashlight and shone it up ahead.

He was in a lava tube. The way ahead sloped sharply downward at a dizzying angle. He would be able to climb back out, of that he was sure, but it would be a chore. He once again thought about his friends and reminded himself it was important that he find whatever lay ahead as quickly as he could, and then make tracks back to the city.

He slid down the steep tube. At the bottom, it angled sharply to the right before opening up into a large chamber.

Stone regained his feet, took two steps inside and shone his light all around.

"My God," he breathed. "It's incredible."

To his left, a strange script covered the wall—some form of hieroglyphics, if he didn't miss his guess. To the right, a map of the earth adorned the smooth stone. Sprinkled throughout were images of pyramids. He saw some in the expected places: Egypt and Central America, but there were many more, some in North America, which he presumed might be Indian mounds, but others were located in surprising places, such as Eastern Europe, Japan, and even Antarctica. Wavy lines radiated outward from all of them, linking up with other pyramids. He had no idea what they meant, but they had to be important. Was this his grandfather's secret? Was this the great danger of which he needed to be aware? Did John Kane seek this knowledge, or did he even know what lay on this island?

He searched the cavern to make certain he had not missed anything, and quickly satisfied himself that the map and strange writing were the secrets intended for his eyes. He drew a pencil and notebook from his rucksack, sat down, and prepared his mind for the task. Once focused, he set to copying the hieroglyphs. His hand zipped across the pages, sketching perfect copies of the symbols at a breakneck pace—another skill he had picked up after his military service. When he'd filled more than twenty pages, he turned and copied the map of the earth.

He sat there, feeling an odd sense of incompleteness. Something was not right. If his grandfather's secret was locked in a map and a set of symbols, why had it been necessary for Stone to come to this place? Couldn't his grandfather have copied them down as Stone had just done? There had to be more. Perhaps there was something to be gained here that could only be experienced.

He laid his pencil and notebook aside, closed his eyes, and calmed his thoughts. He reached out beyond the confines of his body, feeling the energy of the space. Something pulsed in the air...something powerful and deadly. The world map seemed to detach from the wall and drift toward him. Despite his closed eyes, he could see it clearly. It encircled his body and formed a sphere that slowly rotated around him.

Energy seemed to flow up from within the earth into the pyramids. As Stone watched, shadows encroached from all around, and the pyramids began to glow. It soon became evident that the grid formed by the network of pyramids was keeping the darkness at bay.

His eyes snapped open. He stood, his mind alive with the vision he'd just witnessed. He didn't fully understand what he had just seen, but something had changed inside him. What was the darkness the pyramids held at bay, and what was his connection to it? He hoped the secret lay in the hieroglyphs, or perhaps buried in his subconscious. Somehow, he felt as if knowledge had seeped inside him, insinuating itself into the deepest recesses of his mind. But he could spare no time now to figure it all out. He needed to get back to Trinity and his friends.

26– THE BATTLE

Stone heard the commotion long before he reached the valley. Alarmed shouts, sharp commands, and loud cracks and crashes emanated from far below. He quickened his pace, and the noises solidified into the unmistakable sounds of battle. His heart raced. What had happened? Were Trinity and the others all right?

He shot down the steep path at full speed. Several times, he almost lost his footing but managed to remain upright. A fall down the steep, rocky face of the volcano could be deadly, but he did not consider the risk. He'd left his friends alone and now he feared they were paying the price.

He topped a rise and Ogygia came into view. Down below, the Ogygians battled the caveman-like Varri. Stone searched the chaos for signs of his friends and quickly spotted Moses, who had presumably emptied his pistol and now fought with a cudgel in one hand and his machete in the other, battering and slashing the powerful but slow Varri. Nearby, Alex had found a spear and was desperately trying to keep a determined Varri at bay.

He saw no sign of Trinity.

It felt like an eternity before he finally burst into the city and into the midst of the battle. He drew his Webley, dropped to one knee, and selected his target—a brute of a warrior, armed with two clubs, who was driving Alex backward, in Stone's direction. He took careful aim and squeezed off a single shot that whizzed past Alex's ear and took the huge Varri in the eye socket.

Alex whirled about and a relieved grin spread across his face.

"Stone! Thank God. We're being pressed hard here, and Moses and I are out of bullets. Not to mention, I'm no great shakes at hand-to-hand fighting." For emphasis, he shook the spear he carried.

"Just stay alive. Where's Trinity?"

Alex's eyes narrowed. "I haven't seen her since the attack began. We were at the pyramid, meeting with the council. All of a sudden, people started crying out, and the next thing we knew, the Varri were among us. Moses and I drew our pistols and ran outside. Samman followed us, and for a moment, I was sure he was going to attack me; there was something in his eyes. He gave my pistol an odd look, like he was about to be sick, and then the Varri were on us, and I lost sight of him."

"And you don't know what happened to Trinity?"

"When the Varri closed in, Samman shouted something about the council keeping her safe."

Stone immediately took off for the pyramid, weaving around the combatants who dueled all around him. A Varri occasionally blocked his path, but they all fell to Stone's bullets. By the time he reached the pyramid, he'd reloaded twice and was down to four bullets in the revolver.

The battle raged hottest at the foot of the pyramid. Malik and Akente fought like cornered tigers, slashing and thrusting their spears at every Varri that came within reach. Stone prayed Trinity was safe inside, but he'd have to fight through the throng in order to find out.

Forsaking his Webley in the close quarters, he took up a club dropped by a fallen Varri, drew his knife, and drove forward. The Varri fell back before his furious attack. He killed a few, but most shied away.

He heard a cry in the distance and saw Moses leading a group of Ogygians. Their line swept in behind the Varri, who were attacking the pyramid. On the pyramid's heights, a group of young men armed with bows seemed to take heart from this new turn of events, and began loosing arrows at a rapid clip.

The Varri assault crumbled, and soon the brutes were in full retreat. Stone, Moses, and Akente held back as the Ogygians drove their enemies from the valley, taking down as many of the fleeing primitives as they could.

Stone watched the retreat for a few seconds, and then turned to Akente.

"Where is Trinity? Is she inside?"

Akente's brow furrowed. "She retreated toward the back of the city when the attack began." He pointed his lips in the direction from which Stone had come. "I believe Samman was with her."

"I came from that direction and I didn't see her." Stone paused. "Why would Samman take her? Why wouldn't he stay and fight?"

"At the time, I thought he wanted to keep her safe. Of course, I was busy battling for my life, so I did not think about it for very long. Now, it seems odd. The pyramid would have been the safest place for her."

"Samman is a traitor!" a voice called. Stone turned to see four Ogygian warriors escorting a bound Varri in their direction. "This one," he prodded the Varri with his spear, "says Samman let them in."

Akente muttered something that must have been an Ogygian curse and stamped his foot.

A heavy feeling hung in the pit of Stone's stomach. "Do you have any idea where he might have taken her?"

Akente shook his head.

"We'll just have to find her, then," Moses said.

"Find who?" Alex, still clutching the spear, appeared around the corner of the temple. Other than a bruised cheek and a few cuts in his forearms, he appeared unscathed.

"Trinity," Stone said. "Samman took her."

"Where? Why?" Alex asked.

"I know where," a small voice from somewhere above them said.

Stone looked up to see one of the young archers looking down at them. "I saw Samman running away with the white woman."

"Did you see where they went?" Akente demanded.

"Yes." The dark-skinned youth paused and swallowed hard. He turned and pointed with his lips. "They went that way. He took her down the Path of the Dead."

"No." Akente took a step back. "It is forbidden."

The youth shrugged.

"The Path of the Dead? What does that mean?" Stone asked.

"It means." Akente took a deep breath. "That Samman has taken Trinity into the Arena of Souls."

27- THE ARENA

"What is the Arena of Souls?" Stone demanded. His fists clenched, he took a threatening step toward Akente, who backed away.

"A place few go, and even fewer return. No one speaks of what happens there." Akente glanced nervously about. "It is also the path your grandfather traveled in order to leave the island. At least, the last time anyone saw him, he was entering the arena. We assumed he had died, until you arrived with news of his safe return home."

"Why would Samman take Trinity into this Arena?" Alex asked.

Akente grimaced. "Samman has entered the Arena many times. Inside there, he is a master; perhaps the most powerful of us all. I imagine he took the woman there because he knows no one will follow him."

"He was wrong on that score," Stone said. "Show me the way."

"You cannot. You are from the outside, and you know nothing of the arena, nor what waits there for you." Akente looked to Alex and Moses, a pleading expression on his face, but both remained silent. "If you go in, nephew, you will surely die."

"My grandfather, your father, was an outsider, and he didn't die." Stone seized Akente by the shoulders and resisted the urge to shake him like a rag doll. He had no desire to harm his uncle, but he was not to be deterred, not when Trinity was in danger. "Besides, it doesn't matter how dangerous it might be. I abandoned by friends once for the sake of this island and my grandfather's secret, and look what happened. I'm going in no matter what, so you might as well show me the way and tell me anything you can of what I should expect. If I'm going to bring Trinity back alive, I'll need all the help I can get."

Akente stiffened. For a moment, Stone thought his uncle meant to resist, but then the man nodded. "Follow me." Stone released his grip and Akente led them back in the direction of the volcano.

"I am not permitted to tell you what I experienced the only time I ventured into the arena. Do not bother trying to force me. I would die first."

Stone could tell Akente was serious, so he did not press the matter. "Go on."

"I will say only that many dangers await you there. It is well known. But the dangers are not mere physical threats. You must be strong in mind, body, and spirit in order to survive."

"You said Stone's grandfather escaped the island by going into the arena," Alex said. "Obviously you don't know how he survived, but do you have any idea as to how he got off the island?"

"I cannot say for certain, but I can guess." Akente hesitated and then looked around to see if anyone stood within earshot, but everyone appeared busy, either tending the wounded or patrolling in case the Varri returned. "I should not say this, but there is a place in the arena where the water meets the land. There are many boats there. The waves are fierce, but if you can make it beyond them, the current will pull you out to sea."

"Like a riptide," Moses said.

"How do you know about the current?" Stone asked.

Akente shook his head. "I have said too much already. There is the way into the arena." He pointed to a tiny stream that trickled past their feet and over a rock ledge into a bowl-shaped canyon. A curtain of mist concealed the canyon floor from sight, with only the tops of a few trees jutting out of the blanket of gray.

Stone turned to Alex and Moses. "Wait here. I'll get Trinity, and then I'll come back for you and we'll find the way out together."

"We're going with you," Moses said.

Alex nodded in agreement. "Whether we go with you now or after you find Trinity, we're going to have to pass through the arena in order to find the beach Akente described. We might as well go along now and try to be of some help. After all, we *are* in this together."

Stone didn't like it, but it made sense. He turned and peered over the edge of the waterfall down into the mist. "How do we get down there?"

"You stand in the water at the edge of the cliff," Akente said. "And you jump."

Stone nodded. "I probably won't see you again," he said to Akente. "Thank you for your help, Uncle."

"I wish you well, Nephew." Without further word, Akente turned and walked away.

"No time like the present. Let's get on with it." Stone turned and leapt out over the edge.

He did not experience the familiar, tingling sensation associated with falling. Instead, the mist that shrouded the arena seemed to bear him gently down until he hit the water.

He scarcely felt the impact, and his body made no splash, as far as he could tell, and the water felt strangely warm. He slid beneath the surface and immediately began swimming as fast as he could. He expected Alex and Moses to follow any second, and he didn't want to be underneath one or both of them when they hit the water.

Surfacing, he found himself in a large pond, or tiny lake, depending on one's perspective. The mist hung like a thick blanket about fifteen feet overhead. Here and there, pillars of mist whirled like tiny tornadoes, putting him to mind of marble columns supporting a low roof. Rocky paths wound through the sparse trees and tropical foliage, but despite the terrain, the place felt artificial, like an odd sort of temple. The shore, a rocky, gray ledge, lay about thirty feet away, and he struck out for it, ignoring the uneasy feeling with which this place filled him.

On the shore, he scanned the ground and quickly found scuff marks that he took to be tracks left by Trinity. He had no doubt Samman could have moved through this landscape without leaving a sign, but Trinity was a city girl and was probably fighting her captor all the way. Now that he had a trail, he waited with rising impatience until he saw his friends plunge into the water. He quietly called out to them and they swam over. After hauling them out of the water with ease, he led them into the arena.

He ran as fast as he could while still watching for signs. Trinity had left regular scuff marks along the way, and in a few spots it was obvious she had dug in her heels and forced Samman to drag her. He smiled at the thought, and then wondered why Samman had not merely thrown her over his shoulder and carried her. Perhaps he *wanted* to leave a trail? Of course he did. The arena was his home field, as the ballplayers might say, and Stone was a rookie. Here, Samman had all the advantages. Or so he believed, which could work to Stone's advantage.

Off to their left, one of the columns of mist began to whirl faster, then broke off and spun toward them. Having already plunged through the thick mist during his descent, Stone doubted it would do them any harm, but he saw no reason to take a chance.

"Look out on the left," he called back to his friends and quickened his pace. He heard the sound of rapid footfalls behind him, and then Alex cried out in alarm.

Stone looked back to see his friend sprawled face-down. A rope of mist wrapped around Alex's ankle like a snare, and tendrils of mist sprang forth and began creeping up his leg.

Moses drew his machete and slashed at the mist, but it re-formed as soon as it parted.

Not knowing what else to do, Stone grabbed Alex by the wrists and pulled. The mist held on, stretching like rubber as Stone hauled Alex farther away. The mist now reached halfway up Alex's body and his eyes suddenly went wide. He opened his mouth as if to scream, but made no sound.

Desperate, Stone lifted his friend bodily off the ground, and the mist released him.

"Let's get out of here," he said to Moses. "I'll carry Alex until he can run again."

"I...can...manage..." Alex shuddered with each syllable, like a man coming in from the cold.

"Are you injured?"

"No." Alex would say no more.

Stone put him down and eyed him doubtfully, but Alex immediately set off at a slow jog. Stone again moved to the fore and was relieved to find they had not lost the trail.

As they ran, they narrowly avoided several more attacks from the columns of mist. Soon, Stone realized that the path they followed gradually spiraled inward.

"I think this path will lead us to the center of the arena," he said.

"How...can you be...sure?" Moses panted. Though Moses was in good physical condition, the exertion was taking its toll on him.

"I'm not completely certain, but we've already circled the arena once. It appears to be taking us ever closer to the center as we go. We might be better off..."

He didn't see the coil of mist that whipped out across the path like a tripwire, snaring him and Moses, and sending him plunging to the ground.

28- THE MIST

A **bitter cold** enveloped him like he had plunged into a frozen lake. This was nothing like the warmth he'd felt when he descended through the mist. It had been an illusion—a trap baited by an otherworldly predator. He struggled to regain his feet, but his limbs were numb. And he was drifting...

A ghostly figure approached. Unable to move, Stone watched as it broke through a column of mist, and gained form. It was his grandfather!

Despite his years, Samuel Stone stood tall, his posture rigid, his eyes brimming with vitality, and his face twisted in a disapproving frown.

"I needed you and you weren't there."

"What?" Stone battled the confused thoughts that whirled in his mind. He had to get back to his feet and find Trinity. She was somewhere in the...

Where was she? At the newspaper, he supposed, working on another story. He'd see her earlier this evening. His grandfather paced back and forth across his study, while Stone sat rigidly upright in an uncomfortable chair.

"I thought you were the one person I could count on," Samuel continued, "but you left, and you didn't come back."

"I'm sorry, Grandfather. I had things to do." But what

were *those things, exactly? Stone found he couldn't recall exactly where he'd gone and what he'd done since leaving the army. Why hadn't he come home sooner? He'd had a reason, of that he was certain, but what was that reason?*

"I hope they were important things." Samuel shook his fist in Stone's face. "Because now I'm dead!"

"What are you talking about?" Stone asked. But, as he spoke, his grandfather fell to the floor. "Grandfather!" Stone shouted. He dropped to the floor at Samuel's side and felt for a pulse, but if it was there, it was too faint to detect. "I'll get you to a hospital." He doubted his grandfather could hear him, or that he was even alive, but he swept the surprisingly light old man up in his arms and sprinted to the front door.

As he stepped out into the damp, cool air, he felt his burden suddenly grown lighter. He looked down and gasped. Samuel's body withered before his eyes, and then crumbled to dust. Before Stone could comprehend what had happened, a loud shriek of tires split the air, followed by a resounding crash.

He turned in the direction of the sound and the sight turned his guts to water. His father's car sat crushed against the bole of an old oak tree. Steam poured from under the hood and climbed upward in whirling columns of mist to join the fog that rolled in off the Potomac.

Stone dashed full-speed toward the site of the accident. He could see two figures slumped forward inside the vehicle— his mother and father! He wanted to call to them, but something held his chest and throat in a vise grip.

He reached the car and tried to pull the door open,

but the impact had crumpled the front end and the crushing effect sealed the door firmly shut. He ran to the passenger side but found that door similarly wedged closed.

Inside, his mother raised her head and looked at him through glassy eyes. "Brock?" she mouthed.

"I'm going to break the window!" Stone shouted. "Put your head down."

His mother shook her head. "You're too late. You should have been here sooner."

"Mother, put your head down!" Stone drew his fist back to punch the glass, but the car began to change. He stepped back and looked on in amazement as the vehicle, like his grandfather's body, cracked and began to fall apart.

Faintly, he heard his mother say, "You didn't come home. Now we're dead, and Trinity has been taken. Where were you?"

The car crumbled into dust, but the last three words hung in the air.

"Where were you?"

Where had he been? And what was that about Trinity being taken? Yes, she had been taken. But that couldn't be right. He had just gotten home, so how would he know? But somehow, the knowledge was there, inside his head.

He ran toward the house, determined to hop on his motorcycle and head off in search of her, but where would he start? It didn't matter. He would go looking for her and trust that the knowledge, which he was now certain lay buried deep in his memory, would return. He had to find her. He had been gone too long, and now his family was dead. So few of the people he loved remained. He wouldn't fail again. He couldn't. Guilt and remorse swelled up inside him, so powerful it threatened to overcome him.

As he flew past the window to his grandfather's study, he stole a glance inside. Something told him that, as foolish as it seemed, the answer lay inside. Had his grandfather known who took Trinity? He ran to the window. He'd only take a moment. He could spare that much. But as he looked around, a dark cloud of despair descended over him. His selfishness had caused all of this and now there was nothing he could do to fix it. His parents and grandfather were dead, and nothing could bring them back from that, and Trinity, vanished without a clue. It was useless. He was useless. He should give up and die.

His knees buckled and he hit the ground, lacking the strength to rise. His body felt cold and numb, as if he stood on the edge of hypothermia. It didn't matter anymore. He didn't matter. He would do the world a great service and lie here until he turned to dust like the people he cared about. He was less than useless.

The fog rolled in thicker now, turning the world white. Perhaps he was already dead. Somewhere in the distance, he heard faint cries. The voices were familiar. Alex? Moses? Maybe they knew where Trinity was. Perhaps hope remained. With a greater effort than he had ever made in his life, he climbed to his feet and sagged against the windowsill. He'd catch his breath and then go in search of his friends.

His tired eyes drifted to the study. He scanned the desk, the rows of books, the walls; nothing lay there that told him where he could find Trinity. Not the old maps of the world that hung on the far wall. Not the huge painting of Everest that dominated the space behind his grandfather's desk.

Something clicked in his mind. Everest. Tibet.

Now he remembered where he'd been. Memories flooded into him as the dam inside his head burst.

He'd run miles through the snow in his bare feet, scaled dizzying heights without rope or gear, swum frozen rivers, carried burdens that would have crushed another man, fought hand-to-hand against men who could leap and somersault with superhuman ability, men whose hands, feet, knees, elbows, even their fingers were deadly weapons. He'd learned to live, even thrive, in the frigid climate and rarified air of the highest peaks.

But the most difficult thing he'd learned to do was control his mind. He'd learned to sharpen his focus to a needle point, setting aside all the horrors of war he'd witnessed, all the guilt and remorse he felt for the things he'd done in service to his country. He'd spent hours contemplating a single dust mote, a flake of snow, a whisper of wind. He had become more than he had ever been before.

Suddenly, he knew exactly where he was and what he had to do. He was not in Virginia. He was in the Arena of Souls, where the greatest peril lay not in threats to his body, but to his mind. He sat down on the imagined grass if his grandfather's lawn and focused his mind.

It was not easy. He felt the icy chill of the mist all around him, heard his friends' voices, and fought the doubt that threatened to pull him back to unreality.

Slowly, surely, he shut it all out, drawing his focus on the only thing that mattered: completing the task at hand. He gathered his strength and his will, and as he did, he pushed back against the oppressive cold.

Warmth returned to his body and clarity to his mind. With a forceful swipe of his hand, he hurled back the veil of deception and stood once again in the Arena of Souls.

Before him, Alex struggled to lift the heavier Moses off the ground and break the connection as Stone had done for him.

His full strength now coursing through him, Stone swept Moses up, breaking the grip of the mist.

"My pappy," Moses gasped, "I left him alone. He died all alone without me there."

"I know," Stone said. "The mist plays with your mind. It takes your guilt and insecurities and cripples you with them."

"What do we do?" Alex asked.

"I can't teach you in a few minutes what it took me years to learn, but perhaps I can help you. Think about the very best thing about you— the thing that matters the most to those who care about you. Focus on it. Fill your mind with it and don't let go. And while you're at it, do your best to stay away from the mist and help one another if you get caught up. Keep following the path. If you don't catch up with me, I'll come back for you. Just hold on. Don't let it win."

"Where are you going?" Alex asked.

"I'm headed for the center of the arena, but I'm going to take a shortcut."

29- THE ALTAR

Stone stepped off the path and headed for the center of the arena. All around, columns of mist converged on him, but he moved too fast for most of them to reach him before he flew on by. Occasionally, one would reach out with a foggy tendril, seeking to grab hold of him, but he leapt through them. Their touch chilled him to the bone, but he scarcely felt it, so concentrated was his will and so focused was he on his goal. Nothing could deter him, and he would not let the sinister magic of this place make him doubt himself again.

Up ahead, the mist began to clear, and he found himself standing before a ring of stone triptychs. For a brief instant, he wondered if he'd been transported to Stonehenge, but he quickly noticed that, unlike its European counterpart, this place was fully intact. Each stone was pristine, set firmly in its place, and cut with a precision worthy of the great pyramids of Egypt.

At the center of the ring, Samman stood behind a stone altar, his thickly muscled arms folded across his broad chest. Trinity lay writhing atop the altar. She wasn't held down by ropes, but tendrils of mist.

Stone didn't hesitate. He stopped, drew his Webley, and took aim. He was a crack shot and the distance would be no problem for him, familiar as he was with this weapon.

He squeezed the trigger.

Nothing.

"Your weapons do not work here," Samman called. "You cannot even pick up a rock and strike me with it. The arena would turn your blow."

Stone had no reason to doubt the man's words. "I don't need a weapon." He continued to stride toward the altar.

Samman smirked. "We shall find out soon enough. You are swift, but you cannot outrun the mists inside the circle. They answer my call."

So, Samman didn't suspect that Stone could resist the power of the arena. He would have to use that to his favor.

"I just might be faster than you think."

"Perhaps," Samman said, "but can you outrun the mists while carrying your woman? I assure you she is in no condition to move on her own."

"What do you want with her? She's done nothing to you. I'm the one who brought her here."

"It is not a question of blame. I hate all outsiders, as I hate all Ogygians who allow outsiders to enter our city. So, I must kill you." Samman glanced down at Trinity. "All of you."

"If you were going to kill her, you would have done it already." Stone hoped that was true.

"I will see to her after she has watched me kill you. It seems you are a source of hope and resolve for her, and a defiant spirit will not increase my power. She must submit to my will before she dies. Only then, I may control her spirit in the arena."

Stone narrowed his eyes. "You've killed in the arena before."

"You are not as foolish as I thought. It is true. Many

of the men who ventured here might have survived, but I made sure they did not. By breaking their spirits before death, I control them. It is the nature of the Arena of Souls. Soon my power will be so great that it will extend beyond the arena, and I can wield it in Ogygia. Then I shall bend them to my will." He paused. "I dared not try to kill your friends during the battle as I had originally planned. They were armed and there were too many witnesses about. I will, instead, deal with them after you are dead. I assume you brought them into the arena with you?" He grinned.

Stone had heard enough. He had to get to Samman before the man realized that Stone could not be affected by the mist. Once he made that realization, Trinity would be the only leverage he had, and there was no telling what he might do. If his power in the arena was as great as he claimed, he might be able to kill her before Stone could do anything about it.

Stone charged forward. Immediately, Samman sent tendrils of mist whipping out at him. Stone cried out in feigned shock and surprise, and leapt to the side. As the tendrils flayed him, he staggered and whirled about, batting at them as if he could knock them away.

"You remain on your feet," Samman said in the clinical tone of a zoologist discussing the behavior of a wild animal. "That is more than I expected, but this is only a fraction of my power." He raised his hands above his head and the tendrils dissipated, as did those torturing Trinity. She sat up weakly on the altar, saw Stone, and cried out.

"Brock! Get out of here! Leave me!" Even in the face of terror and impending death, she remained courageous.

Samman swept his hands in a wide arc, and a dozen ghostly figures appeared behind him.

Despite their vaporous forms, Stone could tell they were natives. These must be the spirits of the men Samman had killed. He had only an instant to register this thought before the ghostly figures charged him.

Despite the utter control he held over his mind, he felt the spirits' touch. Each seemed to burn his flesh as they collided with him. His grunts of pain were genuine, and it took all his strength to remain on his feet, staggering to and fro, each stumble bringing him closer to the altar.

Trinity continued to call his name, her cries causing him greater pain than the assaults by his ethereal attackers.

"Do not despair," Samman said over the sounds of their voices. "You should take pride in how well he is doing. No man ever stood up to my attacks as long as he has. Of course, it must end soon."

The icy streaks of pain that striped his flesh intensified. Stone brought his hands up to cover his face and began to thrash around. He reeled toward the sound of Trinity's voice until he felt his foot strike the altar.

He opened his eyes to see Samman standing before him. Shock registered on Samman's face as Stone struck him full force on the chin. The spirits faded into nothingness as Samman wobbled backward. Stone pursued him, lashing out with a series of kicks and punches that put him down on his hands and knees.

"Mercy," he pleaded. "I am beaten."

Stone hesitated. He knew he should finish it—end Samman's life so he could never kill again, but to kill a surrendering enemy went against everything he believed in. He'd seen enough of that in the Great War.

"Kill him, Stone," Alex said. He and Moses had made it to the arena. "Then get us out of here. Neither of us has much left." Beside him, Moses leaned against a triptych, breathing heavily.

For an instant, Stone wondered if he could carry Samman back to Ogygia to face justice and still make it back in time to get his friends to safety, but he couldn't bear the thought of leaving them behind again.

"I…"

He was spared the necessity of making a decision when Trinity stepped forward and smashed Samman's temple with a stone the size of her head.

"I guess he was lying about the arena turning rocks aside." She dropped the stone on the ground alongside Samman's lifeless body and brushed her hands on her pant legs. "I thought you were a goner for sure, but you were faking, weren't you? How did you manage?"

Stone quickly explained how he and the others had managed to stave off the worst effects of this valley of the dead.

Trinity swallowed hard. "I'll try it. Now, how do we get out of here?"

"According to Akente, there's one way off this island." Stone scanned the horizon, but the cloud of mist obscured the skyline. He pictured his grandfather's map in his mind and immediately identified a natural harbor at the island's northwest corner. He didn't need to see the sky to know which direction to go, and he led his friends in a straight line toward that spot.

Ten minutes later, the mist suddenly ended at a row of alien-looking trees. In the distance, the water of the harbor sparkled in the sunlight.

"Thank you, Lord." Moses dropped to one knee and slumped over, gasping for breath. Beside him, Alex sank to the ground, similarly exhausted.

"What now?" Trinity rested her head against Stone's chest, and he wrapped her in a tight embrace.

Before he could reply, Trinity shrieked. All around them, the trees had come to life. The closest one leaned toward them, its giant leaves opening up to reveal a blood-red mouth lined with green, teeth-like spikes. He had been mistaken. They weren't trees at all.

"Venus flytraps!" He drew his hunting knife and sliced a clean gash through the mouth of the flytrap. The entire plant shuddered, and then attacked with fury. He leapt backward and felt an icy shock. They were pinned between the deadly mist and the carnivorous plants. "Follow me!" He took Trinity by the hand and ran along the line of writhing, hungry flora. Moses and Alex drew their machetes and hacked away at the plants as they ran.

At the end of the cluster of flytraps, they hit a sheer rock ledge that ran all the way to the water. It was the end of the line. Time for what Trinity would call an act of heroism though he considered it more an act of desperation. Stone sheathed his knife and turned to the others.

"Give me the machetes and get ready to run for the beach when I give the word." Moses and Alex appeared too tired to argue. They surrendered the long blades with barely a word of protest.

"Whatever happens, don't try to help me. I want you two to get Trinity home safely. The thing that matters most to me is that the three of you survive, and hopefully continue on the path my grandfather set for me." He slid his rucksack off his shoulder and handed it to Trinity. "I wish I had time to explain, but what's inside might be of more importance than any of us could imagine."

"I understand." Trinity's eyes glistened with unshed tears. She kissed him gently and then stepped back. "Give 'em hell, big boy."

Stone grimaced and turned to face the last Venus flytrap. Its mouths opened and snapped closed again only feet from where he stood.

"Ready?" He tensed and then leapt forward, whirling the machetes in a blur of flashing steel. He slashed and parried, slicing through the gaping maws. He moved on instinct, his muscles flowing into the forms of the sword dances he had learned from the Tibetan monks. The attack slowed, and he called out to his friends, "Now!"

The flytrap sprang back to life and Stone moved like a caravan guard, putting his body and blades between the predator and his friends. The spikes scored his flesh as he fought with concentrated fury. Behind him, Trinity shrieked and Alex cursed loudly. Stone moved toward the sound, hacking away. One of the mouths snapped closed inches from his knee, and he dodged, slamming into the rock ledge. He wouldn't last much longer.

"We're through!" Moses shouted. "Come on!"

Stone dove forward toward the base of the deadly plant, rolled, and came up on the balls of his feet. He leapt toward the beach and the last remaining mouth snapped closed on empty air where his foot had been an instant before. He felt sand beneath him and cool salt air against his cheeks and he knew he was free.

Trinity ran to embrace him, but pushed him away.

"You're all bloody," she said. "Let me see." He permitted her to inspect his wounds, and she soon proclaimed him fit for travel. "Nothing too serious." Her countenance suddenly darkened. "Alex is another story."

A few feet away, Alex lay on the sand while Moses bound Alex's wrist with strips of cloth he'd torn from his shirt. Blood soaked the fabric. Stone's heart fell at the sight.

"He's gonna need a tourniquet," Moses said. "That thing done bit his hand clean off."

Stone knelt alongside his friend. "Alex, I'm so sorry. I don't have the words."

Dazed from the shock of his wound, Alex looked up at him through glassy eyes. "It's all right," he grunted. "I've always wanted a hook hand. Like the pirates we used to pretend to be down at the river when we were kids."

Stone almost managed a smile.

"Just wrap me up and let me rest while you figure out our next move."

"I think the next move is obvious," Trinity said.

All around lay the wreckage of various ships, boats, and rafts. Stone recognized a Viking longboat, a Phoenician hippoi, even a Civil War-era ironclad—all victims of the Triangle, swept to this place by whatever mysterious forces controlled this part of the sea.

"I think that one will fit the bill." He pointed to a wooden lifeboat that sat on the shore as if left there just for them. The craft appeared to be in immaculate condition: the rudder and oars were in place, and its white paint gleamed in the sun. A red flag with a white star was emblazoned on each side of the stern—the emblem of White Star Line, the oceanic navigation company. Above the flag on the port side was the word "Liverpool." On the starboard side…

"SS *Titanic*," Trinity whispered.

"Well, I'll be John Brown," Moses murmured.

Alex opened his eyes and squinted at the boat. "I hope that isn't an omen."

"The ship sank, but this boat made it all the way here," Stone said. "I'll take that as a good sign."

An hour later, their boat, still anchored off the coast, appeared on the horizon.

"Almost there," Alex murmured. He lay slumped against the gunwale while Trinity manned the rudder, and Stone and Moses hauled at the oars.

"Well, Mister Brock Stone," Trinity began, "what are you going to do when we finally make it home? Going to disappear again?"

Stone shook his head. "Not exactly, but I have a feeling I'll be doing a lot of traveling in the future." He described what he had seen in the cave, finishing with his conclusion that some undiscovered…power, for lack of a better term, posed a threat to the world. "I don't know what that threat is, or what it all means, but my grandfather clearly took it seriously, and he believed I could do something about it." He turned to Trinity. "I guess this means you won't be seeing much of me."

"Not so fast." She raised her index finger. "I'm in this now. Where you go, I go."

"Same goes for me," Moses said.

"I'll lend a hand." Alex raised his bandaged stump. "Wait, I don't seem to have one to spare."

Despite his reservations, Stone had to laugh.

Whatever faced him in the future, it was good to know he wouldn't be alone.

The End

If you enjoyed *Arena of Souls*, give *Track of the Beast* at try. Bigfoot, the Illuminati, a Jefferson-era conspiracy, and more!.

Want to keep up with David and his work? Sign up for his mailing list and receive a free ebook collection! Visit his website at www.davidwoodweb.com.

ABOUT THE AUTHOR

David Wood is the author of the popular action-adventure series, The Dane Maddock Adventures, as well as several stand-alone works and two series for young adults. Under his David Debord pen name he is the author of the Absent Gods fantasy series. When not writing, he co-hosts the Authorcast podcast. David and his family live in Santa Fe, New Mexico. Visit him online at www.davidwoodweb.com.

Made in the USA
Monee, IL
30 April 2021